# Edge of Heaven

## PG Forte

*"I ain't got no more worries*
*I'm gonna spend some time with you*
*Loving you takes such courage*
*Everyone's got their eyes on you."*

—George Michael, *The Edge of Heaven*

# Prologue

People have all sorts of misconceptions about angels. They think we're perfect. They think we don't have feelings or emotions or lust after each other's bodies — and occasionally after yours as well. That's nonsense. Of course we do. We're only human, after all. Or at least some of us were. Once.

My name is Edge. I'm an angel. And this is my story.

I understand how confusing it might seem at first, all the questions you're probably asking yourself. Like aren't angels and humans fundamentally different? Aren't we completely separate species? Weren't angels created first? The simple answer to all those questions is yes. But whoever said the universe was simple?

There's nothing uncomplicated about the human heart. There's nothing easy when it comes to free will. If you consider all the trouble a soul can get itself into, or if you think about all the tasks the celestial hosts are called on to perform, you'll see why it only makes good sense for there to be more than one type of angel in the world. Besides, if you'd ever caught even a glimpse of one of the seraphim — those fierce and fearsome creatures forever on fire to do battle against the forces of darkness — you'd think twice too about using them as messengers to ordinary people. Never mind sending one of them to stand watch over the kiddies while they sleep!

The path to becoming an angel is actually far easier than you might imagine. All you have to do is lose your soul. That's another concept many people find difficult to grasp. Soul loss. It's something else that comes entirely too easily to most of us. Sudden death, violence, a lack of closure, guilt—that's all it takes sometimes. You lose your way. You disconnect. Your soul fractures. The next thing you know, you're waking up here. Stuck in limbo. Unable to move on to heaven...or the next plane of existence...your next lifetime...

Okay, you want the truth? We don't really know where we're supposed to go from here. All we know is we aren't going anywhere. Not yet. Not until we've found our closure, mended our fences, or in some cases, performed a truly unselfish act.

Unselfish. Now that's hard.

Most of the folks here don't have it as tough as that. They've just got closure issues to deal with. Closure is a piece of cake. It's something almost anyone can manage once they're ready for it. I've seen people find closure in the damnedest things. But unselfish acts—truly unselfish acts? Well, that's a whole nother story.

Take me, for example. I committed suicide. That's what landed me here. And you really can't get much more self-absorbed than that.

# Chapter One

Hands down, Matteo Matinucci has to be the sorriest-looking angel I've ever seen. And if there's one thing I've seen my fair share of during my stay here in limbo, it's disenchanted newbie angels in training. More than my fair share, if you really want to know, 'cause ever since I screwed the pooch with the special angel in charge of assignments, helping the new recruits settle in is the only work I ever seem to get.

The rookie du jour is standing on a pier at sunset, looking out over a lake, when I arrive for our meet and greet, and since it's nowhere I've ever been before, I have to assume this is someplace he's remembering. Of course, everything here is basically an illusion anyway. This isn't really a pier, just like that's not really the sun out there, disappearing behind the pine trees, but that's not what's important right now. Real or imagined, the echo of my footfalls, loud against the old wooden planks, drifts out over the still water as I amble along the boardwalk. He turns at the sound. The minute our eyes lock I know I'm in trouble.

Are those tears I'm seeing? Yep, I'm pretty sure they are, and the thought of playing damp shoulder to one of the newly departed does not improve my mood by one iota.

He shakes his hair back from his face and blinks once or twice like a man waking up from a very deep dream. A faint flush mounts his cheeks. Those glistening eyes narrow slightly. Other than that, his puppy-dog gaze never wavers as I shorten the distance between us. My steps finally falter under the weight of that unsmiling amber stare. The smile I'd plastered on my own face falls away. I clear my throat but still have trouble getting the words out with anything like my usual cool nonchalance. "Hey there. You must be Matteo."

I'm used to my new charges looking lost and alone, used to them looking scared or confused, but this one... Damned if it doesn't look like he's discovered a whole new subbasement level to gut-wrenchingly distraught. The pain and longing in his expression hit me like a fist. A big part of me wants nothing more than to fold my arms around him and promise things'll get better. Never mind that the saner parts think popping him one instead—demanding he man up and stop sniveling—would be a far better way to play this. I mean, what call's he got to look so damned depressed? Sure, he's dead, and I know that disappoints a lot of people, but it's still no cause for the abject despair he's radiating.

He's not in hell, all right? Things could be worse.

Determined to try again. I paste my smile back in place, extend my hand. "So, Matteo, right? Or do you prefer Matt?"

"Call me Mattie," he says, relief painting his features as he finally comes unstuck. His hair swings forward again as he lunges enthusiastically for my hand. I feel a shock of recognition when strong fingers wrap mine. He folds my hand up with both of his and hangs on for dear life. Once again our gazes collide, and I find myself staring, unable to look away.

Mostly I'm hung up on the name thing. Call him Mattie? Like hell. That's a kid's name. The kind of name any self-respecting guy should have outgrown by the time he turned eight. There's a tense sensation in the pit of my belly, a spreading tightness in my chest, a sudden snugness in my jeans, and I can't account for any of it—until the press of his fingers on mine finally registers in my brain.

Oh, holy shit. We're holding hands? Still? Not cool.

I pry myself free and take a step back, feeling instantly a whole lot better now that I've put some distance between us. I shove my hands in my pockets—just to keep them out of harm's way—take a deep breath, and try again. "Good to meet you, Matt. I'm Edge. I'm the angel assigned to help you settle in."

Matteo looks me up and down with altogether too much warmth, igniting an interest I do not want to feel.

"You're an angel?" There's a fair amount of skepticism in his tone, but at least he appears to be perking up a bit. I figure that's a good thing. "And your name is Edge? Seriously? What kind of name is that? Is it short for something?"

Can you believe this shit? I'm getting crap about my name from a guy with a handle I wouldn't give my pet Pekingese. Not that I'd ever be caught dead with a Pekingese. No pun intended. "It's not short for anything, all right, pal? It's just my name." And speaking of names, he is damned well going to have to get used to being called something other than Mattie. At least while he's under my wing.

His eyes glimmer. A smile starts licking at the corners of his mouth. The look he's giving me creeps me out. It's a little too knowledgeable, a little too understanding, and far too wise for his years, which I'd put at around mid to late twenties or roughly the same age I was when I'd kicked it. The big difference between us being I've been stuck here on the astral for far too long. I've earned all of my wisdom and understanding. The hard way.

But never mind that. What I really want to know is what's with the smile? What the hell does he have to smile about all of a sudden? And why like that?

"There's gotta be more to it, right?" Matteo says teasingly. "So is Edge your first name? Your last name? What's the rest of it? Come on, you can tell me. It's not a secret, is it?"

He powers up the wattage on that damn smile until he's wearing a look that's 100 percent pure wickedness. It puts an unholy twinkle in his eyes. It brings his dimples out of hiding and makes it that much harder to look away.

Oh, fuck me. Is he flirting with me? Not cool at all. My chest is so constricted I can hardly get my next words out. "The name's Edge." I want to cringe at the sound of my own voice: husky, rasping, gravelly, thick. "Just Edge."

The dimples deepen; so does his voice. "Edge. Just Edge," he repeats in an uncanny imitation of my own gruff tones. "Oh, man, how double-oh adorable is that? Okay, handsome, I'll bite. What do I have to do to get you to tell me the rest of it?"

"There is no rest of it." Edge had been my surname in life—you can blame my great-grandfather and the good folks at Ellis Island for that one. In death… Let's just say it's the only name I care to use. "Let's change the subject, shall we? You've probably already figured out I'm here to teach you the ropes, right?"

"Ooh, ropes." Matteo's eyes light up. He smiles eagerly. "Sounds kinky. Are we talking Shibari or straight-up bondage?"

"What did you say?"

"Sorry, Master Edge. Yes, please, sir, teach me about ropes."

"All right, that's enough." I know it's my own fault. I just had to go and mention ropes, didn't I? But all the same... Shit, I cannot believe he went there. For a moment, I'm lost in the imagery his words have conjured. My face starts to flame. My guts get so twisted up with shame I think I'm gonna puke. "You cut the crap right now. You hear me, kid? Just shut the fuck up."

Matteo's head snaps back, and I don't think he'd look any more surprised if I slapped him in the face with a dead fish. His smile dissolves. The tears reappear. "Sorry," he mutters, glancing away, gazing out over the water again.

He's looking and sounding just as miserably unhappy as he was when I first showed up, and I'm ready to put my fist through a wall. *Crap.* I rake my fingers through my hair, stare at him in frustrated silence. I'm unable to think of a single thing to say. Which is more than I can say for Mr. Sunshine here. Figures the guy would be a talker.

"Oh, hey, look, man, I'm sorry, all right? I-I didn't mean anything by it, I swear. I just thought maybe... Oh, shit. This is real. Isn't it? I mean, it's really happening? It's not a dream? I was hoping —"

"Yeah, it's real, all right." As his words register, my fists unclench. He thought he was dreaming? Well, that explains a few things, doesn't it? It's an understandable mistake. Apparently, it feels like that for a lot of us at first. It seems no one's ever happy to get the news their lives have ended, but their issues remain.

So okay. No reason to freak out. Guy was simply in denial for a minute there. I guess I'm cool with that. That's something I can deal with, something I can understand. Something I have a much more than passing acquaintance with myself, if you really want to know. And now that we've gotten that straightened out, maybe we can get ourselves back on track and get down to business.

It's kind of a compliment, you know? I should probably be feeling all sorts of flattered that he'd accepted me so readily as part of his horny fantasy, his own personal dream angel. I smile to show him there's no hard feelings. "Baby, this here is about as real as it gets."

Baby? The word hangs in the ether between us. Now who needs a punch in the mouth, huh? Just where in the hell did that come from?

Matteo seems not to have noticed the endearment. "I just... I can't believe I'm dead," he says, his voice a sad little whisper. "I didn't really get a chance to do...anything. And now it's over. It's really, truly over?"

There's a question mark at the end of his last sentence — I can hear it — and I know we're not quite out of the denial woods yet. Reaching over, I pat his shoulder consolingly, ignoring the urge to really, truly pull him in for a quick hug instead. "Sucks, don't it? But don't you worry. It's gonna be okay, you know? We'll put you straight in no time."

"Straight?" Matteo gives me a watery smile. "Never really thought of that as an option."

"That's not... Shit. I didn't mean..."

"I know. I was just kidding." But there's no amusement in his gaze. I feel my throat begin to close up again. "Thank you...Edge."

"Not necessary," I answer quickly—while I can still speak. "I'm just doing my job."

# Chapter Two

I can see I'm getting ahead of myself. How do I describe this place in a way you'll understand? Being in limbo... Well, it's a lot like being booked for an indefinite stay at a very exclusive executive retreat. Sure, it's posh, it's peaceful, it's pleasant. It's just about anything you want it to be, within limits. But there's a reason why heaven's called heaven and limbo...is not.

It's all just a little too bland here, a little too remote. There's this sense of being isolated, of being out of touch that you never quite get used to. Just like you can never completely lose the feeling that you've been cut off from something pretty damn important. Even if you're not quite certain what that something is.

It might take you a while to notice that last part, though. If you're a new arrival in limbo, I can guarantee you the first thought in your mind is not gonna be, How can I keep busy? Stay long enough, however, and that'll change. Time doesn't exactly pass here in what I like to call never-never land—it just is. But all the same, with nothing but your own sorry thoughts to occupy your mind, eternity has a way of weighing on your spirits after a while. To say nothing of the way all that peacefulness gets to wearing on your nerves.

Luckily, there's no shortage of tasks we angels are called upon to perform—from the very simple, such as finding lost keys or arranging for an open parking space, to the more profound. Keeping vigil in hospitals and at deathbeds. Riding shotgun in emergency vehicles. Providing comfort for the grieving and protection for those in danger.

While we're generally happy to be of service in any way we can, I'd be lying if I said there weren't some jobs we prefer more than others and some assignments we'd just as soon they give someone else. Pulling the kind of duty I'm stuck with now, just one step removed from babysitting and a big, fat goose egg on the adrenaline-pumping scale—it irks. I can't help thinking my talents could be better utilized doing something else, and not to put too fine a point on it or anything, it's a bit of a time waster. I can't see how holding the hand of yet another fledgling angel is ever gonna help me move ahead.

Not that there's anything ordinary about this particular fledgling. He's like a shiny new penny in a pocketful of change. Bright. Untarnished. Makes me wonder how he ended up in limbo at all.

"So, Matt, do you have any idea where we are right now?" It's a baseline question, one I ask all the newbies I work with. Their answers give me an idea of how much work I'm going to have to put in, how much resistance I'll have to overcome.

He looks surprised, but he nods all the same. "Sure. This is the lake where I used to spend my summers as a kid. My family used to have a cottage right over there." He nods toward the shoreline and frowns. "No, wait. That's not right."

I follow his gaze, taking in the picture-perfect Craftsman-style cottage, all cedar shake and river rock and shiny white trim. "Nice."

"Yeah, but it's not right, though," he repeats, sounding puzzled and not a little sad all over again. "It burned down...several years ago. I was away at school. I'd wanted to squeeze an extra semester in that summer. The rest of my family—they were all here when it happened. My parents. Both of my sisters. Everyone but me."

Ah, shit. Way to go, Edge, I think, watching as the cottage changes. Now it's a blackened hulk, blanketed with ashes, wreathed in smoke. This is what he chose to remember? I'm not sure what to make of that. Most folks here aren't ready to confront their issues this quickly—if ever. I lay a hand on his shoulder. "Okay, look, we can take this as slow as you need to. We don't have to do this right now."

"No, that's okay." Matt's still staring at the remains of the cottage, his expression resigned. "It is what it is, right? Nothing lasts forever."

"Well, some things do," I correct. "Just not so much on the earthly plane."

He shoots a sharp glance in my direction. "We're not there anymore, are we?" he asks, once again catching on a lot quicker than most. "So what is this place—really?"

"It can be anyplace you want it to be." I figure he could use a breather, so I wave the burned-out cottage away with a thought. Now it's a bar I like to frequent out in the Sonoran Desert. Papa Joe's. And yes, I said frequent. Present tense. You think we don't need a drink now and then? We do.

"How'd you do that?" Matt says, frowning suspiciously at me.

I flash him a wry smile. "Welcome to the afterlife. Let me buy you a drink, and we'll talk about it."

"Buy me a drink?" he repeats in surprise. "The afterlife requires cash? Man, that's a bummer."

"Just a figure of speech." I motion for him to follow me. "C'mon, let's go."

"Wait." Matt glances down. There's hard-packed earth beneath his feet now rather than wooden planks, and at first I think that's what he's looking at. But then he raises his head. "I don't think I'm dressed right for a place like that."

Surprised, I look him over. There's certainly nothing wrong with his appearance. I mean, angels tend to be pretty easy on the eyes in general, one of the perks, I guess, but even so, this is one good-looking kid. Broad shoulders—even I can't help but notice those. He's slim and fit and decently muscled. He's got dark blond hair, sun streaked, maybe a little too long, and gold-hued skin with just a dusting of hair along his forearms and on his legs.

Even if the way he's dressed—in shorts and a loose tank top, like maybe he'd just got done playing beach volleyball when he died—wasn't a tip-off, I still would've known from his skin color alone that he must have spent a good part of his time on Earth outdoors. That healthy a glow was never a gift from the tanning-bed gods.

"This isn't Earth," I remind him. "Appearances don't matter. No one really cares how you dress here."

While we're on the subject of appearances, let me say something about clothes. We're angels, all right? We're not ghosts. We're not stuck in the same clothes we were wearing when we died. We put on our pants one leg at a time just like anybody else.

When we're on assignment back on Earth, we dress to fit in. When we're here, we dress however we like. Usually, that means wearing the kind of clothes we felt most comfortable wearing in life. In my case that'd be jeans, a T-shirt, leather jacket, and a pair of boots — nicely broken in. But we get all types here, and like I said, no one ever thinks too much about it.

Matt shakes his head. "Well, I care."

Eyes narrowed, he studies me in silence. I fidget restlessly. "What are you doing?" I ask, but in that same instant I have my answer. My own eyes widen as I take in his altered appearance. His clothes are now a near match for mine; only the jacket is missing. "That really wasn't necessary." And it really shouldn't be possible either — not for someone so new. "But not bad. Good job."

"Thanks."

I nod. There is only one fault I can find, and it hardly bears mentioning, but he could have opted for a slightly larger T-shirt, one that doesn't hug the muscles of his chest and arms quite so tightly. I tear my gaze away from the span of his shoulders before I can become too distracted and gesture at the bar. "You coming with me?"

That unsettling glint is back in his eyes. "I sure hope so."

"What?"

"Never mind." Flashing an easy smile, he closes the distance between us. "Tell me about this place," he says as we cross the deserted parking lot. "Is it someplace that was important to you in life?"

So now he's asking the questions? I don't think so. I shake my head. "Nope. I'd been long dead when I discovered Joe's. I just like it, you know?" Oddly enough, I always felt more at home here than I'd ever felt in any of my actual homes. "I spent some time here during a couple of my first missions back on Earth." A couple of my first and last Earth missions, I should have said, since those days seem to be over. I can't quite keep from sighing at the thought. I was good at those assignments.

"You seem a little down about that, babe," Matt says as he beats me to the door. He holds it open and motions for me to precede him. "I'm guessing they didn't turn out so well?"

I glare at him over my shoulder. "They turned out fine." I was *damned* good at those assignments. Not that it's any of his business. And since when did I become his "babe"?

Inside Joe's, it's quiet and completely empty. Well, what did you expect? We can't create people, you know. Objects, yes. Memories, sure. But living creatures are beyond our abilities, which makes total sense when you think about it. The possibilities for abuse are endless and so horrifying that even the semblances—automatons, golems, graven images, clones—are strictly *verboten*. Still, it looks like a bar, it smells like a bar, and that's all that really matters.

"What're you drinking?" I ask as I materialize a scotch and soda for myself.

Matt gazes thoughtfully at me for a moment then shrugs. "Beer, I guess."

I make him a glass and push it across the bar to him.

He tastes it and smiles. "Not bad."

Satisfied, I nod. Not bad at all. I take a sip of scotch—and nearly spit it out again when he reaches past me to dip his hand casually into a bowl of pretzels that weren't there a moment ago. I stare at him hard.

How the hell is he doing this?

"So you were going to tell me about this place," Matt says, still smiling as he munches on his pretzels. "Somehow I'm not seeing this as heaven, and even though you're temptation personified, I imagine hell overall would be a lot more unpleasant. So where are we?"

"We're in limbo," I answer, ignoring the "temptation" line. "Sometimes when people die, they still have issues to work out—problems that keep their souls from going to heaven right away. Limbo is kind of a way station. It's the place where all that stuff gets resolved."

Matt gapes at me with something like disbelief. "So you're saying what exactly? We're gay boys with issues? That's why we're here?"

"I'm not saying anything of the kind." I ignore the "gay boys" line too. "I don't know what sort of issues you've got, and I don't really care. The fact that you're here speaks for itself." I swallow some more scotch. "Look, you want some advice? Don't beat yourself up too much about them, whatever they are. Guilt's too easy a trap to fall into. And while a little denial is understandable, it'll definitely slow things down for you. You'll make better progress once you stop making excuses and accept that you're here for a reason."

Matt nods. "Makes sense. So what are your issues?"

"They're none of your damn business." My issues? What are we talking about my issues for? I'm here to help him. That's kind of enough for me to deal with right now. "Do not go there. *Capisci?*"

"Whoa. Dude, chill." Matt lifts his hands in a gesture of surrender. "I'm just making conversation. I'm new to the whole postmortem dating scene, remember? How'm I supposed to know what lines not to cross?"

"Dating?" Now that one I can't ignore. "What the fuck, man? This is *not* a date."

"Coulda fooled me." Matt's eyes grow hot as he looks me over, as he flashes another of those wicked smiles my way. "You pick me up, invite me out, buy me a drink. What am I supposed to think?"

"Something else," I say, feeling more than a little shaken as I refill my glass. And no, we can't get drunk, if you're wondering, no matter how much we drink. Sometimes I really wish that weren't the case. I can hear the unsteady note in my voice. I can feel the tension in my chest, my groin. "Something different."

Matteo's smile widens. He shifts a little closer. "You sure about that?"

I shake my head. "Not a date."

# Chapter Three

As soon as I get a chance, I make an excuse to get away. I need some time to myself. I need some space. Even more importantly, I need help.

There's only one person I can think of who might actually be able to do something about this mess I'm in: Sophia, the angel who gave me my start when I arrived here, the one who helped me pull myself together and find my feet. Sophia knows things. She's damn near omniscient. I don't know how long she's been here—a long time, I'm guessing—but probably not quite as long as she likes to suggest. She always says she's been here from the start, that she had a hand in building this place. I'm pretty sure that's just showing off.

She's reclining on a pile of cushions beneath a gauzy canopy, eating dates out of a silver bowl, when I find her. It's the kind of lush, fantastic setting that practically begs for mostly naked, sloe-eyed slave boys wielding palm-frond fans. Not that you'd ever find that kind of thing here, of course. The slaves, I mean. Palm trees we got in abundance if you want 'em—witness the dates. But the afterlife is essentially a slave-free zone.

"I need you, Soph," I say, sinking down onto the cushions to sit beside her and reaching for her hand. "You have to help me."

She doesn't answer right away. Her eyes, so dark they're more purple-black than brown, are agleam with…something. Amusement? Mischief? Sympathy? Spite? Hell if I know.

She looks me over thoughtfully—not unlike the

way Matteo's been doing—the fingers of her free hand toying with one of the glossy black curls that cascade over her shoulders. Between the hair and the eyes and the slightly Roman nose and that flowing white robe she's wearing, she looks like she just stepped off a piece of Etruscan pottery. So, okay, maybe she has been here for kind of a while. No matter. Angels don't age. Have I mentioned that already?

For the most part, we all look pretty much like we did when we were alive, maybe a little bit better, with any design flaws corrected, any damage repaired. The usual default age for angels is twenty-nine. If you died at fifty, you'll look twenty-nine here. If you died at ninety, you'll still look twenty-nine. If you see one of us looking much younger that that, we're likely here as the result of some kind of tragedy—accident, misadventure, malfeasance, stupidity.

"What is it you wish me to do, love?" Sophia asks, finally breaking the silence. And isn't that a fine question?

"Get me reassigned?" Now that I'm thinking about it, I don't know exactly what I want her to do. I hadn't really thought that far ahead. I figured she'd tell me. "Or I dunno, find someone else to take over this bullshit job they just stuck me with? Help me get this damn newbie off my back?"

Her eyes widen in surprise, and it's obvious this was not the answer she'd been expecting. She slips her hand from mine. "Why come to me? You know I have nothing to do with assigning tasks."

"No. That'd be Lorraine." I can't keep the bitterness out of my voice. "Come on, Soph, you know I can't go to her with this."

Lorraine. Now there was a mistake. Which is exactly what Sophia warned me would be the case. But had I listened? Do I ever? I half expect her to say *I told you so*, but she doesn't. She doesn't say anything at all. Then again, she doesn't really have to.

"She's doing it out of spite, Soph. You know it as well as I do, and that's not fair to the kid. He's a good guy, you know? Anyone can see that. I don't even know why they sent him here. But he doesn't deserve to get sucked into our battle. How can she even do that? Aren't there rules about that kind of thing?"

Sophia frowns. "You don't really believe that, do you?"

Her question catches me off guard. "Sure I do. Which part?"

"All of it," she snaps, sounding more impatient than I've ever known her to be. "I'm surprised at you. You know better."

"I know better? Since when? You should've seen him. He's a mess. He was bawling his eyes out." A slight exaggeration, I know. But there were tears.

"And it made you uncomfortable. Is that what this is about?" Sophia's smiling again; full, lush lips curved upward into a look so impossibly ambiguous the Mona Lisa should take notes. She leans forward, then lightly traces the line of my jaw. "Why is that? This isn't the first time that's happened, is it? Grief. Remorse. Confusion. Regret. They're all part of the process sometimes. You of all people should know that."

Me of all people? Yeah, that's great. Isn't that just like a woman? Throwing your weaknesses back in your face every chance she gets. "I'm not you, all right?

If I was, maybe I'd know how to handle something like this. Look…why can't you help him?"

"Me?"

"Sure," I reply, warming to the idea. "Why not? How hard could it be? After all, you helped me, and this guy—I promise, he'll be a walk in the park in comparison." Granted, I don't know this for certain, but after you've been on the job for a while, you begin to develop an instinct for these things. I imagine Matt would be a pleasant enough assignment for most people. He's easygoing, good company, a quick learner, and damned attractive. Just because I don't want to work with him doesn't mean others won't feel differently.

"My poor, poor boy." Sophia rests her forearms on my shoulders. She gazes at me sadly, fingers teasing the hair at my nape. "You do like to make things hard for yourself, don't you?"

Hard? I eye her suspiciously. Actually, I'm trying to make things less hard. Not that I want to go there with her, although I will if I have to. "What else do you have on your plate right now? Maybe we can switch tasks or something. It will be our secret. No one will ever have to know."

Sophia purses her lips in thought. I press my advantage. I shape her waist with my hands and give her a little squeeze, all the while flashing my most persuasive smile. "Come on, what do you say?"

I lean in even closer—close enough to press a soft kiss against her lips. When she doesn't resist, I do it again—harder, deeper, a real kiss this time. She slides her arms around my neck, and I want to sigh in relief.

This is what I've been needing for who knows

how long. Her mouth opens under mine. I feel the faint shimmer as her clothes disappear—and that by itself is almost enough to distract me. I don't know how she does it. Maybe I'm a slow learner, but I still have to take my clothes off the usual way, one piece at a time.

Shoving those thoughts to the back of my mind, I pull her more fully into my arms, thrilling to the soft heat of her skin, the warm, round weight of her. *This* is what I've been wanting—these rolling feminine hills and valleys. Who needs broad shoulders, anyway?

I palm one luscious breast, dip my head to taste the swollen tip. Then I let my hand slide farther south to cup the generous curve of her ass, to coast down the smooth length of her thigh. Her skin like silk, the sweet raspberry nub of her nipple, all the slick softness between her legs—that's what I want. That's all I want. This. Right here. Only this.

"Oh, Edge." With a groan, Sophia pushes me away. Her clothes are back. "You think far too loud," she grumbles. "You always have. That's what got you in trouble with Lorraine in the first place, you know. Also, you protest too much."

"I have no idea what you're talking about." My gaze skims over her gown as I try and get the mood back. Taut nipples poke through the filmy fabric. Her chest rises and falls with every rapid breath. My own breath comes faster once I let the memories rise: Sophia's lips wrapped around my cock, so wet and warm; the whisper-light touch of her fingers skating across my skin. We have a bit of history between us—have I mentioned that fact? "Come on," I tell her. "You want it too."

"I do want it," she answers, still frowning. "The

question is, do you?"

"Of course I want it. What kind of guy do you take me for?" What kind of guy would I be if I didn't want what she's offering?

Sophia shakes her head. "Be honest with me. What did you really come here for? What are you so upset about?" Overhead, the perfect blue sky has gone the slightest bit gray. I feel the hairs lifting on the back of my neck. The clouds are scuttling by a little faster than before as if driven by an otherwise imperceptible wind. Which is especially odd since at the same time the soft breeze that has been gently ruffling Sophia's curls goes absolutely still.

Sophia stares at me intently. The hush that's fallen over the atmosphere grows deeper every second until I can't take any more.

"Sophia, please. I can't do this."

"Oh, Edge." She heaves a sigh, and with that the spell seems to break. The breeze picks up; the clouds slow down; the sky shifts back to blue. Weird. "Why must you make things so complicated? Look...just go and talk to the man. Do it for me. You can do that, can't you?"

"Talk to him?" I don't want to talk to him. And no, actually, I don't think I can just talk to him. I think that fact has been rather firmly established by now. Dating. Jesus. Why the hell did he have to say something like that? Besides, talking — that's what gets you into trouble, you know? Because it so rarely stops there. Talking can lead to all sorts of other stuff, and usually it does. Unbidden, images of just what it could lead to flood my mind. My body shudders, and I honestly can't tell what it is I'm feeling. Anticipation?

Revulsion? Fear? "What am I supposed to talk to him about?"

"About anything! Get to know him. Find out what he likes, what he needs, how he died. Why do I even have to tell you this? This isn't the first time you've dealt with this type of assignment, is it?"

"No, it damn sure isn't." But it's the first time in a long time I've felt this kind of pull, this kind of—oh hell, let's face it—this kind of attraction to another person. Just the thought of him makes me hard—and that scares me shitless. What makes it truly insane is that I know it's not even real.

Sure, he looks good—now. But what are the odds he actually looked that way in life? He was probably more Elephant Man than supermodel. More Richard Simmons than Fabio. Hell, maybe he was Richard Simmons. It would explain the clothes, the maniacal twinkle in his eyes...a lot of things, actually. I make a mental note to check when I get a chance. The truth will set you free. Isn't that what they always claim?

Sophia is watching me expectantly, kind of like she's waiting for something or hoping for something or... Oh, I dunno. Is there some kind of magic word I'm supposed to be saying? Didn't I already say please?

"Look, Soph, why can't you just...you know..." My voice trails off. Shit. Suddenly I'm not sure how to say what I've been thinking. I'm not even sure I want to say it anymore. And that scares me more than anything. I thought I wanted her to do for him what she did for me, but now that I'm finally taking a moment to actually remember everything she did for me...and to me—that we did to each other, my initial thought isn't seeming like such a good idea after all.

Call me selfish; I don't care. It wouldn't be the first time I've heard that, but I'm suddenly not real sure I want to share Sophia with Matt. Or the other way around either—which is so fucked-up, I don't even want to think about what it might mean.

I was a mess when I first got here. I was broken, and if you'd asked me at the time, I would have told you I was beyond repair. I felt wrecked, crippled—even in my nicely upgraded angel suit. All I craved was oblivion. All I wanted was to curl myself up in a ball and die... Except, oh yeah, I'd already done that, and look how well *that* had worked out.

I didn't think I belonged here. I didn't think I deserved a second shot at heaven, and I damn well knew I didn't deserve all the sympathy and compassion Sophia was wasting on my worthless ass. Lucky for me, she thought otherwise.

She brought me back to life. She made me feel whole again. And yes, there was sex involved. Lots of sex. Blisteringly hot angel sex. You have no idea, and I'm not gonna tell you either, because if people knew what they were missing, they'd be dying to get in here, and there's enough people doing that as is it is.

Sophia's eyes have turned sultry, making me wonder if she's been reading my mind and knows what I've been thinking even without my saying it. For a moment, I'm convinced she has. I'm certain she's going to say okay. And what the hell am I supposed to say then?

Instead she laughs—a sexy, semimocking kind of laugh that does nothing to cheer me up. "Don't you think you're leaving out one fairly crucial consideration here? Flattered though I am by your faith in my abilities, I'm not his type."

"Oh, and I am, right?" The instant the words are out of my mouth, I want to bite off my tongue. "Don't answer that." Of course I'm his type. That's precisely the problem, and I'd bet anything that's why Lorraine dreamed this up in the first place—just to mess me up.

Not surprisingly, Sophia disagrees. "You're good at this job. You're a lot better at it than you give yourself credit for. I'm sure that's the real reason Lorraine keeps assigning you cases like these. She knows you'll get the job done, and that makes her look good. The fact that it annoys you is just an added benefit."

But I'm not annoyed. I'm flat-out terrified.

"Sophia, please, I am telling you, I cannot do this. Can't. Do it. I'll fail." I know it in every fiber of my being. "I'll fail, and I'll fall, and I'll take Matt down with me. Is that really what you want?" And then I'll never earn my wings, never get to heaven. Never find a way to put the shame and the pain behind me once and for all.

"Oh, Edge, honey." Sophia smiles sadly. "I know it feels like that." Sitting up a little, she lays a gentle hand against my cheek. "But that more than anything else is exactly why I think you need to try."

***

So, terrific. I'm back at square one. Sophia won't help, and I'm not up to facing Matt alone again yet. But perhaps I don't need to. There's more than one way of skinning this particular cat. I have options when it comes to finding out what Matteo's deal is—how he got here, what kind of issues he might be facing.

Options that don't involve talking. At least not to him. At least not right now. I figure I can learn everything I need to know in the Hall of Records.

Okay, quit laughing.

Yes, it exists, and yes, that's its name. There's a reason clichés become clichés, all right? It's a place, vaguely hall-like, where the records are kept. What else you gonna call it?

You can find pretty much anything you need to know there, about anyone, alive or dead. But "need to know," that's one of the primo criteria for entry. A burning desire for truth and justice will also get you in the door. Idle curiosity won't.

So, my mind made up, I decide to head over to the hall...and nothing happens.

Let me explain one of the more interesting aspects of existence here. Space in never-never land tends to follow the same laws that govern time. In other words, it doesn't really exist either. Everything you need is generally right where you need it, which is usually right where you are too. Makes things pretty interesting, upon occasion, particularly when the thing in question is not an it but a who. But that's beside the point.

The process of getting where you want to go is not quite as automatic as gravity. It requires a certain amount of involvement on your part, but as is the case with many other critical skills—riding a bike, learning to swim, walking through walls—it's not so easy to explain. It's effortless once you know how to do it, impossible until you do. It's less click your heels together and wish, more leap and the net will appear.

Except for times like this when, as I said,

nothing's happening.

It's not the first time I'd known something like this to occur, and I have no reason to suspect it'll be the last, but it's rare enough to be shocking, and it throws me off balance. Like walking into a glass door or getting beaned in the head by a baseball, it's the last thing I'm expecting. For a moment, I forget how to think, and the only noise going on inside my brain can be beautifully summed up in three little letters: w-t-f.

It takes me a couple of instants to recover from the surprise, to fight off the vertigo-induced panic, to pull myself together. I'm shaken, but determined to get back on the horse and try it again. Which I do. Still nothing. Crap.

I want to blame Lorraine for this, but I don't think I can. She's just not that imaginative. Plus I know Sophia's right. It does make Lorraine look good when I do my job well. Sure, she might be willing to trade off a little of that every now and again for the pleasure of watching me crash and burn, but she'd never risk tipping her hand so blatantly.

Besides, Lorraine's a lot like me in one very important respect. We're both extremely determined to move ahead, to do whatever is necessary to get us sent up to heaven, unlike some angels who no longer seem to care whether they ever leave limbo—who've been here so long it seems like home to them. Angels like Sophia, for example.

I don't want to believe it of her, but how can I not? It was her idea that I talk to Matt, that I not give up, that I try—even after I told her I'd never succeed. Maybe she wants me to fail. Maybe she wants me to be stuck here forever. With her. There's a strange pain in the center of my chest as I think about that, accompanied by a been-there, done-that sense of doom. I'm pretty sure it's my heart breaking. All over again.

# Chapter Four

"Is this a bad time?" Matteo asks, showing up on my beach unannounced. He's gazing at me a little uncertainly, and I guess he's responding to the look of shock on my face. At least I hope I look shocked. It'd beat looking panicked, disgusted, and dismayed, which is closer to how I'm really feeling. New as he is, there's no way he should have been able to follow me here, so hell yes, it's a bad time!

"Time doesn't really exist," I say, cleverly sidestepping the question. "And good and bad—those are also illusions."

"I see." Matt's brow crinkles up. He looks around curiously. "So what is this place, anyway, Hindu hell?"

"What? Hell? No, it's not hell, and...why Hindu?"

"Okay, Buddhist maybe. Same basic philosophy, isn't it? Nothing you see is real. It's all illusion, and everything's the same: good and bad, pleasure and pain, action and inaction, blue and green."

I blink at that last part. Now he's got my attention. He's nuts, but he's got my attention. "Uh...blue and green?"

A smile tugs at the corners of his mouth. "Well, yeah, you know, 'cause that's how the world looks, right? From a distance?"

I don't want to do it, but I can't help laughing. "Cute, pal. But I'm pretty sure the Divine Miss M's no Buddhist."

Matteo grins. "My mistake, then." He points at the log on which I'm sitting. "May I?"

I'd like to say no, but I'd have to have a reason to do that. A good reason I mean, one I'd be willing to admit to. Which I don't. "Sure. Help yourself."

It's a big log, practically a whole tree. There's plenty of room for us both. At least that's what I tell myself. Still, it's an effort to keep from moving away. I want to slide over to the very end to make sure he doesn't sit right next to me. Which he does. Big surprise, huh? I don't want to sound like a wuss or anything, but the guy's clearly got no sense of personal boundaries. He's sitting so close to me our shoulders are practically touching. I can feel the heat rising from his skin. It's sensuous, tempting. I have to fight the urge to lean into it.

"So seriously, what is this place?" he asks, surveying the scenery.

I'm kind of wondering about that myself. I mean, I know what I see when I look around me, but I also know it's a reflection of my own thoughts. None of it is actually real. Does Matteo see what I see? Or is he seeing something else? "What does it look like to you?"

He glances around again. "Somewhere along the West Coast would be my guess. Northern California, Pacific Northwest, something like that."

"Yeah, that's how it looks to me too." I stare out at the ocean. Sunlight dances on the waves. A couple of gulls fly by. Who's to say what's real, anyhow? "This is the beach I used to go to as a kid." I point at the rocky shore. "There are tide pools between those rocks. Man, I used to love messing around down there. And over that way" —I turn and point over his shoulder to that place where the beach ends in a fall of boulders and water laps at the base of the cliff—"is the entrance to a cave. It's hard to find. You can only reach it at low tide. Sometimes not even then."

"It seems like all of the best things in life are like that, aren't they?" His voice is low, suggestive. I feel it in the pit of my stomach.

"Like what?"

"Hard to get." He's staring right at me. Our faces are just inches apart. I can see the gold flecks in his dark eyes and the fine gold stubble that lines his jaw. My fingers are tingling. It's like I can already feel the sandpapery texture of his cheek sliding against my open palm. His lips are full, slightly parted. They look soft. They look inviting.

I put my hand in the center of his chest and push. "Tell me more about yourself."

"What do you want to know?" he asks, lips twitching into a tiny smile. "I swear I'm clean. No drugs, no diseases. Or does that even matter here?"

I shake my head. "It's none of my concern. And it's also not what I'm talking about." My hand is still pressed against his heart. He seems not to mind. I do, but I just can't seem to move it away. "Tell me how you died."

And there goes his smile, disappearing in a red-hot instant. He straightens — away from me, away from my hand — and looks out at the water once more. "It was so stupid, you know? So totally senseless."

Oh crap. There's an unmistakable tinge of anger in his voice. Eerily familiar, it puts all my nerves on alert. My heart starts pounding. My jaw gets tight. I don't want to ask it, but it's my job. I have to know. "What did you do?"

"Me? Nothing. It was an accident."

"Yeah, I'm sure it was. So tell me about it."

"Damn car came out of nowhere."

I blink in surprise. "Car?" Okay, not what I was thinking, then.

Matteo nods. "I was out for my morning run along the beach in Santa Monica. Only it was Saturday and I'd slept in, so it was later in the day than I generally go. On my way back, I noticed the stores along the Promenade were open—which they usually aren't when I pass them. There was this kiosk with the cutest baby mobile hanging up in it. My best friend and her partner are trying for a baby. It's been a couple of months, and it hasn't happened yet. It will, though, you know? I mean, they've done all the tests, and there's no reason it shouldn't. I wanted to give them something to help keep their spirits up, and this mobile was so perfect I couldn't resist. I just had to have it. So I crossed the street, and...I was waiting while the sales clerk wrapped it, when it happened."

"When what happened? I thought you were killed by a car?"

"I was. Driver must have had a heart attack or something. Car jumped the curb and plowed right into us. It was my bad luck that I had my back to it at the time. If I'd had a little more warning, I might have had a chance to get out of the way."

"You were hit by a car while you were shopping." It's not really a question—I'm just trying to wrap my mind around the absurdity of the idea. "While you were buying a gift for your friend's baby."

"Yeah. Can you believe it? And now...I'm never even going to see the kid, never know if it's a boy or a girl or what they name it, who it looks like..."

I nod, but I'm not really listening. To be honest, I'm feeling a little bit jealous. My death was stupid and senseless and largely accidental too. I left stuff unfinished. I left people behind. But there's one big difference. My death was my own damn fault.

Matteo sighs. "I was in med school, you know? I was going to be a doctor. I wanted to make a difference in people's lives. How could it be over like this?"

His words startle me out of my own thoughts. Could it really be that simple? "What did you just say?"

Matteo's brow crinkles up in confusion. "I don't know. What did I say?"

"Is that all you're upset about? The fact you left things unfinished?"

"What do you mean, 'Is that all?' I'm only talking about my whole freaking life! That's a hell of a lot, don't you think?"

"Sure," I lie, arranging my features into an expression of sympathy and concern. "Of course it is. It's a lot to take in, a lot to deal with. I get that." Inside, I'm punching the air and cheering wildly. Well, all right. Dude's got closure issues. Halle-freakin'-lujah.

What did I tell you about closure? Easy as pie to deal with once you know what it is you need.

Usually, this kind of assignment is a simple matter of getting the newbie acclimated to his new existence. It's pep talks and hand-holding. It's walking the fledgling through the process—showing him how to move around, acquainting him with the facilities, teaching him how and where to find what he needs. It's boring and repetitive and generally thankless. All I'm really supposed to do is get him to the place where he can start looking for his own answers. Then he's on his own.

That's how it usually works. But not this time.

As of this moment, I'm making it my personal mission to find out just what it'll take to get Matteo Matinucci's ticket punched straight through to heaven. Whatever it is, whatever he needs, whatever I have to do, I'm gonna make it happen—*rapido*.

No way do I want to wait around, wasting time, while Matteo figures things out for himself. A guy like this can't help me. In fact, all he's done since he's been here is make me feel worse about my own situation. I want this guy the hell out of limbo—and out of my hair—like yesterday.

# Chapter Five

"So okay, why don't you tell me about these friends of yours?" I suggest. As focused as Matteo seems to be on the subject, I figure it's as good a place to start as any other. "The ones who you say are trying to start a family."

"Megan and Beth? What do you want to know?"

"I, uh...yeah." Megan and Beth? "Tell me anything. Whatever you want."

Sometimes I forget how much has changed in the years since I've been dead. Sometimes I remember, and it makes me envious. Two girls and they're trying to have a baby together. And apparently, they're not too shy to share all the gory, intimate details with their good old buddy Matt.

How different might my life have turned out if the world I knew had been more like the one Matteo lived in, if the people I'd lived with had been that open, that accepting. I might still be alive if that were the case. Or well, no, maybe not now I wouldn't be. But on the other hand, I might not have been stuck here all this time either.

"You seem to really care about what's happening with them," I say. "Would knowing how they're doing make this transition easier for you?"

Matteo shrugs. "Sure. Of course. I'd love to know how things are going for them. Why wouldn't I?"

"Okay, so tell me about them. Maybe I can help."

He sighs and looks off into the distance. "Well, Meg and I met in high school. We dated for a while, even went to prom together, but that was just because it was easier to pretend than to face the taunts and other crap we knew we'd get if we...you know, came out. We both always knew which way we were wired, but it was our secret. I guess we bonded over the fact that we were both different. By the time we got to college, though, we were ready to stop lying. Meg hooked up with Beth in the middle of sophomore year. They've been together ever since."

"And what about you? Was there a Beth waiting for you in college too?"

The twinkle is back in Matteo's eyes. "You mean did I ever find my special someone? Nope, can't say I did. But it wasn't for lack of trying, I can promise you that."

"So is that part of what you feel you might've missed out on?" I really hope that's not the case. I need this to be simple. Easy. Resolvable. Is that even a word?

Matteo laughs. "Naw, baby, I didn't miss out on a thing. I pretty much shagged my way through college. Safely—I wasn't completely stupid about it— but let's just say my dance card was usually full."

I nod, not trusting myself to talk. Did I mention the envy? Oh yeah, I'm feeling it now, all right. I feel so...cheated. To be honest, there were a couple of guys I knew when I was alive who I wouldn't have minded shagging. Maybe more than a couple. I never let myself, though. I mean, of course I didn't. How could I have? That was never an option for me. It wasn't even a remote possibility. So I'd put it from my mind and...tried other things instead.

"I don't really buy into the theory that there's someone out there for each of us," Matteo says, and if you ask me, he sounds a little wistful. But maybe I'm reading too much into it. "There's something like what—six billion people in the world? And we're each supposed to find just one? What are the chances?"

I shake my head. "I wouldn't even begin to know how to calculate something like that. The universe is such a chaotic mix of missed connections and random coincidence it seems kind of pointless to even try."

"And love at first sight—that's even more far-fetched, don't you think? To fall for someone you don't even know, that's just..."

"Ridiculous."

"Right." Matteo sighs. "So. What now? Where do I go from here?"

I take a deep breath and try to pull my mind back from the abyss. Man, I hate it when the talk gets all metaphysical like this. Where's the benefit, you know? "We don't really know for certain. Most of us believe heaven's our ultimate destination—if we're lucky. But first we have to deal with whatever unresolved issues brought us here."

"Not what I mean." He nods at the beach. "I'm saying, where do I go from *here*? How do I get off this beach? I'm not even sure how I got here in the first place. One minute I was somewhere else, next thing I knew..."

"Well, sure. That kinda thing takes practice. I can't understand how you found your way here either." I'm still a little freaked-out about it, if you must know. No one else has ever managed to track me down like this.

Matteo shrugs. "Must've just got lucky, I guess."

"Yeah, well, luck's not always the best teacher.

That's why every newcomer to limbo is assigned a mentor whose job it is to help them figure things out. Someone who's been here awhile and knows what's what and can help them settle in."

"For real?" He quirks an eyebrow at me and smiles. "I've got my very own guardian angel to watch over me?"

"That's one way of putting it." For a newly dead guy, he sure does smile a lot, which is not altogether a bad thing. It beats the tears, right? But the look in his eyes is pissing me off. He's staring at me expectantly, like any moment I'll start pulling rabbits out of a hat. "What? Why're you looking at me like that?"

"Oh, no reason. But tell me, when do you suppose this angel of mine might be showing up?"

"I already have shown up," I snap, even more annoyed. "I thought we covered this already?"

"So what're you saying, then—you're it? You're the one I've been waiting for?"

I sigh. "Yes, Matteo, that's what I'm saying." I can't even really blame the guy for sounding skeptical. In his place, I'm sure it would seem like a hell of a long shot to me too.

"Okay, good. That's all I wanted to hear."

"Good?"

"Well, yeah. I was hoping that might be the case."

"You were?" I eye him suspiciously, not believing a word. What is he up to? "Why's that?"

"Because." There's a wicked look in his eyes as he twists round to face me. It's exactly the kind of look that makes you remember the devil's an angel too. "Ridiculous or not, there's something that's been driving me nuts ever since we met."

Before I can come up with a response—before I even have a clue what he's planning—damned if he doesn't kiss me. His hand latches on to my shoulder, keeping me still when I would have drawn back. He leans in, slanting his head at the last minute, angling in just right until our lips and noses are so perfectly aligned it's as though we've been doing this all our lives.

Surprise has short-circuited my reasoning. I know this to be true because before I'm even aware of it, I'm kissing him back. It's shock; that's all. A reflex. And maybe a little curiosity. I've been wondering for so long what something like this would be like. I've been wanting it for so long. Craving it, really. And his lips— so warm and gentle at first, so insistent an instant later—how can I resist his lips or the scratchy stubble that surrounds them, so different from anything I've known before? But it's purely shock. Or mostly shock…partially…

Okay, look, the shock's there, all right? It's definitely somewhere in the mix; that's all I'm gonna say.

My body seems to have switched to automatic pilot. Without any encouragement from my brain, my lips part for his tongue. My eyes are closed tight in bliss and denial. The taste and the smell and the feel of him—it's enough to overload my senses, so sweet, so tangy and male. So good. So right.

So…fucking perfect, actually. And who could ever have predicted that would be the case?

I suck on his tongue, pulling it deeper into my mouth. I'm startled by how much I want that, how much I crave the feel of that agile muscle filling my mouth, taking possession of every inch. My hands grope blindly, searching for some way to anchor us together, clutching at his shoulder, his waist, anywhere my fingers can find a purchase.

Matteo sighs against my lips. He shifts a little — is he moving away? Is he breaking this off? I can't be certain, but I'm taking no chances. I tug him closer, canting my head to the side to tempt him with greater access. I shudder in pleasure at the way our bodies fit together. I can't let this end. I won't let it end. Not yet.

Why should I, anyway? It's just a kiss, after all. Innocent. Harmless. Nothing to get too excited about. Just a kiss and yet...my cock swells and throbs, demanding more. Demanding pressure and friction. Movement. Heat. I'm giving serious thought to the idea of tumbling backward into the sand, pulling him down with me, on top of me. My head spins with the thought of how it will feel to be pinned to the ground, helpless beneath his weight. I want that. Oh, how I want that.

I'm breathless and fevered, and suddenly, in the midst of it all, my conscience makes a belated and completely unwelcome appearance.

*Oh, holy crap. What the fuck do you think you're doing? This is a mistake. Stop it.*

Right. A mistake. I knew that.

I start to pull away, only to find that — somehow — Matteo's hand is cupping the back of my neck. How it got there, when it got there, I have no idea. His fingers are tangled up in my hair; they tense as I try to move, tightening their grip. Then his other hand joins the party, caressing my neck, my shoulder. Obviously, he intends to gentle me into staying right where I am.

You might think knowing what he's up to would be enough to cool my blood, to clear my head, to stop my body from responding just like he wants it to, but it's not. Not even close. I exhale on a shudder, let my tongue curl with his, and I'm lost again. This is too good, too right, too fucking sexy. I'm not going anywhere.

And you know what? I'm really kind of okay with that.

*Okay? The hell you are. End this. Now!*

Desperation kicks in and demands I try again. I straight-arm Matteo in the chest, forcing him away. I struggle for the right words. "Stop it," I say. "Enough now." What I really mean is *more*.

Matteo licks his lips. My cock jerks in response. He smiles faintly. "All right, if that's what you want. I just had to be sure."

There's a heated, carnal look to his gaze. It makes me suspicious over the ease with which he's giving in and secretly hopeful his quick capitulation is merely a trick of some sort. I'm teetering on the verge of pulling him back for another kiss. Who's to know? And besides, what would it hurt?

I know I'm probably better off not knowing, but I ask it just the same. "What do you mean? Sure about what?"

"That you feel it too."

It? Oh yeah. I huff out a shaky breath. I'm pretty sure I know what he means by "it," but sometimes — like now — the best answer to give is no answer at all.

Conscience clamps my mouth shut and orders me not to speak. Not. One. Word.

My silence seems to disappoint him. I guess I should have known he wouldn't let me leave it at that. His fingers trace lightly over the line of my jaw. His voice is smooth as syrup. "You do, don't you, Edge? It's not just me imagining things?"

"Imagining things?" I repeat his words blankly, having lost the conversational thread. "You can pretty much count on it. This place is built on imagination." Right now, however, the only thing I'm imagining is how wonderful those fingers would feel skating along the length of my cock. Or better yet, how his tongue would feel...

"Yeah, I get that." Matteo rubs his thumb across my lower lip, and I have to fight against the insane desire to nibble at the tip or maybe suck the whole digit into my mouth. "But not this time, right? This thing between us — crazy as it seems — this is real. You feel it too. I know you do."

I don't answer. There's a ringing in my ears. I'm pretty sure it's the sound of blood leaving my brain. Given the swollen condition of my cock, there's no mystery as to where it's headed. How did this happen? When did I lose control?

"Edge?"

I shake my head. I can't speak. I don't trust myself to. Who knows what I'll end up saying? I glance away, try to focus on the shore, the rocks, the waves, the sky — anything as long as it's not him.

"Tell me you don't want this, and I'll stop."

"It doesn't matter what I want." The words are so painfully true they give me the strength to meet his gaze. "This is as far as it goes, Matt. I mean it."

# Chapter Six

Matteo pulls his hand away from my face and sits back. He frowns crossly at me. "Okay, so what's the problem here? You're not gonna tell me kissing you was wrong, are you? Please don't tell me those zealots back on Earth had it right all along, that God thinks what I feel for you is a sin?"

I'm diverted for a moment. "Are they still saying things like that back there? I thought things had changed?"

"Oh, sure, I suppose it's a little better now than it used to be," he says with a small shrug. "At least in some places. But there's still plenty of hate and ignorance in the world."

I shake my head. "I guess it's true what they say, the more things change, et cetera. But no, of course that's not what I'm saying. This is strictly personal. It's got nothing to do with anything else."

I don't pretend to know what God thinks about anything. I'm not even sure what I think half the time. And when it comes to this particular subject—make that most of the time. Thinking is second only to talking for getting a guy into trouble, anyway. In general, I try to get away with doing as little of either as possible.

Matteo sighs. "Well, that's a relief. So then—"

"We were talking about your friends," I say, cutting him off. "All I have so far are first names. Why don't you tell me the rest?"

"Why don't you tell me something about yourself instead? I'm sure that's much more interesting."

Interesting. That's one word for it. "Thank you

but no. Anyway, why would we talk about me? I'm not the one who's just died."

"Yeah, but you're dead too, right? I mean...aren't you?"

"Yes, but that was a long time ago."

"How long?" Matteo presses. "What happened? How'd you die? Tell me about it."

"No." I don't even have to think about that—not even for an instant. That's one subject I'm never discussing. Ever. I wouldn't even talk to Sophia about it, no matter how hard she pressed me.

"No?" Matteo repeats in disbelief. "That's it? That's all you're going to tell me?"

I nod. "Pretty much."

Matteo's eyes narrow. "Well, I guess you're just a man of few words, aren't you, 'Just Edge'? A regular Austin Powers. An international man of mystery. Is that what it is?"

I have no idea what he's talking about. But I really do want to change the subject. "Look, I'm just trying to help you find out what's happened to your friends. That's all I'm here to do. But maybe that's not important to you anymore?"

"Of course it's important to me."

"You sure? Seems to me we're getting a little sidetracked. I thought maybe you got distracted, maybe you were more focused on something else now." Something like me. It terrifies me how much I want that to be the case, how much I want him to say yes.

His eyes are cold, his voice like ice. "Trust me, I'm not."

"Good to know." I regroup and try again. "Okay, so getting back to Megan and Beth. Which of them is going to be the mommy?"

"Both of them," he snaps, a not-too-pleased expression on his face. "Their kid's gonna have two mommies. You got a problem with that?"

"Me? Not a bit. Two moms are better'n none, right? But that's not what I'm asking. Which one is actually giving birth?"

He hesitates. I wait. I know he doesn't want to speak civilly to me. I get that. It's what I want too—an end to all the teasing, all the playfulness, a return to business. It's better that way.

Finally, he shrugs in defeat. "Meg," he says on a weary sigh.

This time it's Matteo who studies the beach, and if I had the presence of mind necessary to concentrate on anything else right now, I might want to follow up on that, find out what's making him avoid my gaze all of a sudden. Instead I rein in my curiosity and remind myself to keep the target in sight. The last thing either of us needs is to let ourselves get distracted.

"Meg. Okay, good." I was hoping that was the case. She's the one he seems to have the strongest connection with, which should make it all the easier to track her.

"Yeah, I mean...I think they both want to at some point, but Meg's the one who's trying to get pregnant. Or was. I guess..." He shakes his head, looking even sadder than before. "Maybe she's not anymore. Maybe she's changed her mind or something."

I clasp his shoulder. "Well, let's find out. All right? What I need you to do right now is to focus your thoughts. Keep Meg uppermost in your mind. Think about how important it is for you to know what she's been up to. Can you do that for me?"

Matteo nods. He's watching me closely again, but this time it's okay. This time—if everything works like it should—I'll be doing something even better than pulling rabbits from a hat. I take a deep breath and concentrate on marrying Matteo's need to know about his friend with my own vision of where he can find the information. I watch with pleased satisfaction as the beach starts to shimmer and change, and the marble walls of the Hall of Records rise up to close around us. Ha! I guess Sophia didn't think of this approach when she locked me out.

"Whoa." Matteo's muffled exclamation makes me smile.

I have to admit it is an impressive sight— especially at first glance—with its vaulted ceiling, its terrazzo floor, the gleaming alabaster shelves, and heavy leather-bound tomes. The atmosphere is hushed, solemn—a cross between a cathedral, a mausoleum, and that first breathless pause right after a ball is hit so sweetly you just know it's going to be a home run. "You like?"

"That's some trick."

"Yep. And that's just for starters." I rub my hands together. "All righty, then. Megan—what's her last name?"

"O'Connell," Mattco answers, still gazing around. "This place is…big."

Big is an understatement. He has no idea how vast the hall really is. As a matter of fact, I have no idea how vast it is either. There are records here on everyone who's ever lived or is ever going to.

"C'mon," I say as I head off toward the O stacks. It's not so far from the M's, and if I get a little time, I'm thinking I might check them out too while I'm here. No knowing when I'll be able to get back in on my own.

Our footsteps echo loudly as we cross the floor, and Matteo keeps lagging behind, looking around. I've already found what we're looking for by the time he catches up with me.

"Look," I tell him, pointing to the pertinent entry. "See here? It says she had the baby last May seventeenth. A little girl. Matilda Rose. Eight pounds, eight ounces—"

"What?" Matteo looks startled. "No. That's impossible. What are you talking about? What do you mean she had the baby? I just saw her a couple of days ago. She's not even pregnant yet."

"I know it probably feels like it's only been a few days," I say in my most soothing tones. "But time doesn't pass here the same way it does on Earth. When you die so suddenly, sometimes it puts you into a state that resembles unconsciousness. It can take you a while to recover. Weeks. Months. Years for some of us."

"That's so wrong," he whispers, staring at the vellum page, running his fingers back and forth along the sinuous black script as though his touch could change the words that are written there.

His reaction confuses me. "I thought you'd be happy. Isn't this what you wanted for her? She's moved on. Now you can too."

Matt nods, but the look on his face is furtive, guilty, and sad. It's a look I recognize, one I know very well. "I know I said that," he whispers at last. "And I meant it, or at least I thought I did. But...it was supposed to be mine. I was going to be the sperm donor. I think Beth would have preferred an anonymous donor, but Meg didn't want that. She didn't want to go to a stranger for something like this. She said she wanted it to be someone she knew, someone she cared about. She didn't want her kid growing up without ever knowing his father—but that's just what happened anyway, isn't it?"

He turns to me, his expression so sad it's heartbreaking. *Way to go, Edge.* This is not the face of a man on the brink of closure.

"I told them both I was cool with whatever they wanted. I said I totally understood it was going to be their baby, not mine. I said I was happy just being the favorite uncle—the one who'd spoil the kid rotten, the one who'd get to feed it sugar and send it home. But I was lying. What I was really thinking was that this was the only chance I'd ever have to get my family back, to have a kid of my own. You know? Isn't that what everyone wants—to know that when you're gone, it's not altogether over? That you've left a little piece of yourself behind, that you've made a difference in someone's life?"

I want to say no, because, well, no, actually, I don't believe reproduction is at the top of everyone's wish list. It didn't even make the cut on mine. But even more importantly, I've known a lot of folks who made a difference in people's lives—in all the worst possible ways. People who'd had kids and fucked them up, who probably shouldn't have been allowed to reproduce in the first place.

Something tells me that would never have been the case with Matteo. I'm betting he would have been a good parent. That his kids would have been proud of him and proud of themselves, however they turned out to be. Which is not something everyone can say.

"Look, she named the baby Matilda." I'm grasping at straws, but what else can I do? "She probably calls her Mattie. She named her after you, Matt. Doesn't that count for something?"

Matteo shrugs. "A little. Maybe. But no, actually, it doesn't. Not really. I was going to be the baby's daddy, and I was going to enjoy the hell out of it. Now I'm just... I don't know what I am. Some sort of ghost, I guess."

Icy fingers whisper along my spine. Memories crowd in. They leave me shivering. "Don't say that," I snap at him. "You hear me? You're not a ghost, damn it."

Don't let anyone ever tell you there aren't ghosts. They're the real lost souls, the ones who never properly recover from the shock of their deaths. They don't know who or what—or even where—they are. They have no hope. That's the major difference between us and them. No matter how close to impossible our situation may appear to be, everyone here in limbo knows there's at least a chance we can someday move on. At least, we believe that's the way things work. How could it not? What kind of benevolent deity would tempt us with the possibility of a heaven that exists forever out of reach?

"Well, what am I, then? I'm not alive. I'm not a ghost—"

"You're an angel. Or an almost angel, an angel in training—whatever you want to call it—just like all of us here. That's something to be proud of."

Matteo shakes his head. "Is it? I'm not so sure. I know I don't feel like that's what I am. And I'm certain I don't belong here."

"Of course you do." I step closer, close enough to lay a comforting hand on his shoulder. "C'mon, of course you belong here. You just need a chance to adjust; that's all. Everything's still new to you yet. Give yourself a break, all right? You're only just starting out. No one feels ready for it at first. I know I didn't. It takes a while. Sometimes it takes a long while."

"What if it takes forever? What if I never feel ready?"

"Stop thinking like that. Everyone gets there eventually, and someone like you... It won't take any time at all. You get the hang of things faster than most. I've seen it, Matt. I know what I'm talking about. Besides, you don't really believe the Man Upstairs would make that kind of mistake, do you? If you're here at all, you're here for a reason. You have to know that's true. And you have to know that whatever help you need to reach your goals, it's available to you."

"Is it?"

*Uh-oh.* The hopeful curve of his lips, the sudden sparkle in his eyes sets off alarm bells in my mind. His voice is barely a whisper, yet there's something about his tone... I let my hand drop to my side. *Crap, what have I said now?* "Matt..." We're so close. I should be backing up or pushing him away. I don't do either.

"I need that connection, Edge. You know what I'm talking about, don't you? I need to feel less alone. I need to feel...alive."

Right. Don't we all? "I can't help you with that," I tell him.

"Oh, Edge." Matt shakes his head. "Of course you could. If you wanted to. In fact, I think you might be the only one who could right now." He reaches out and touches my face again, gently, tentatively. I shudder in response, skin flushing on contact. "Please don't say no again."

I gaze at him helplessly. My mouth is so dry I can't speak—not that I have a clue what I'd say at this point. I'm excited and terrified and exhilarated all at once. My body is on fire with anticipation. My heart is pounding, and my cock—well, that's so hard I wouldn't be surprised if it tore right through my jeans.

He moves a half step closer, and I swear my lungs seize. I can't believe this is happening. I can't believe I'm doing nothing to stop it. Don't ever let anyone tell you there's no devil either. He's that soft voice whispering in your ear, the one that says, "You know you want to" at all the worst, most impossible times. Like right now, for instance.

No, my conscience tells me. No way. Don't even think about it, fella. You are not doing this.

Oh, but I know I am.

# Chapter Seven

Matt runs his fingers along my jaw. My heart is racing, but this time I don't resist the caress. His eyes are hot on my face as he slides a cautious hand to the back of my neck. We've been here before. My heart beats faster at the thought. And knowing he means to draw me in for another kiss, I beat him to it. Grabbing hold of his shirt, I yank him forward. He dips his head; I lift my face. There's an instant of confusion as we jockey for position, but finally our mouths connect. Lips parting. Tongues touching. Breath mingling. He sighs with something that sounds a lot like relief, and it's all I can do to keep from whimpering in response. This time I want more than a taste. This time I want everything. I want it all. To hell with the consequences.

As I press him closer, I sense the shift beginning. The space around us alters, and the hall disappears. I don't know where we're going, and I truly don't care. It's Matteo who breaks the kiss, eyes wide with surprise. "Where are we now? Edge, what is this place?"

I cast a quick appraising glance at our surroundings. We're in a bedroom—which doesn't exactly surprise me—and a damn nice one too from what I can see of it. "Beats me. Don't you know?"

He shakes his head. "No. Why would I? I mean, it looks a little familiar, I guess, but not really."

"Interesting." I take another look. The bed is huge. It completely dominates the room—much in the same way the idea of what we're about to do dominates my thoughts. It doesn't take a genius to make the connection—to guess which of us is responsible for that part of the illusion. Embarrassed, I pull my gaze away from it. Through an open archway, I catch a glimpse of marble and tile from what I can only assume is a sunken tub. Everything is decorated in rich shades of burgundy, chocolate, and gold lit by firelight from an immense stone fireplace, and if all that sounds like it might be a little over the top, a little too gaudy or girlie, I'm describing it wrong.

Because it's not like that. Not at all. It's just warm and comfortable and solid. It feels right—just like all of this does. It feels like home, except it's nowhere I've ever seen and a lot nicer than most of the places I've been. "I guess it's ours, then."

"What do you mean 'it's ours'? How can it be ours? That would kind of imply there's an us…wouldn't it?"

Again with the talking? I bite back a sigh. Having finally made up my mind to do this, I'd really appreciate it if we could get on with it before I come to my senses and try and back out of the deal. "Don't read so much into it. All I meant was that it's probably our combined thoughts that created everything here rather than just one of us alone."

He gazes around again. "So…we did this? Together?"

"Pretty much."

"With our thoughts? Like with the drinks and the pretzels and the clothes…only more so?"

"Pretty much." I run my hands over his chest, getting a charge from the illicit thrill of touching him like this. I know it's okay. I know it's what we came here for, but it still feels just as wrong as it feels right.

"And it's ours? Meaning we can do whatever we

want here?"

A shudder runs through me. "Whatever we want. Yes." His words echo in my mind. If that's not an invitation to sin, I don't know what is. Images fill my head, thoughts of everything that simple phrase could possibly contain. My cock pulses impatiently. I clear my throat. "That kinda would be the general idea."

"Well, okay, then." Smiling, he leans in and nuzzles my neck, nips sharply at my earlobe, and suddenly I'm shaking all over. Is it longing? Excitement? Fear? Maybe it's all three.

Now it's my hand cupping his neck as I try to drag him in for another kiss. I want to plunge my tongue into his mouth, search out that elusive, intoxicating flavor—the only thing I know for certain will calm my nerves. He shrugs off my hold and cradles my face in his hands instead. He swipes his tongue across my lips, then kisses me. Soft. Sweet. Almost chaste. Frustrated, I groan his name, cursing helplessly when I'm blasted by another wave of heat. It's not enough. I need more of him. Now. My hands close on his hips, and I try to jerk him closer.

"Easy there," he whispers, a hint of laughter in his voice. "Slow down."

I breathe his name again—more growl than groan this time. I can't do slow right now. I can't do chaste or soft or easy or sweet or anything else that'll leave me with time to think. I'm not really sure how far we're going to take this. Considering the state of my nerves, I count that as a good thing. I don't want to think.

Do I need this? Yes. Do I want it? Hell if I know.

To be honest, I'm not altogether certain I'm

ready. I'm not sure I want to learn the answer to the question, what have I been missing all this time? Will it solve anything? Do I even have a choice?

"Matt, please." I'm begging now—and not just with words but with the tone of my voice, the rocking of my hips. He'd have to be deaf, blind, and stupid not to notice. "Please...please..."

"Shh." He turns my face to the side, his jaw brushing mine. The scrape of our beards spreads heat and electricity all through me. For just an instant I wonder that we don't strike sparks off each other and spontaneously combust. "Let's enjoy this, all right? Can't we take our time and explore a little?"

I swallow hard as his tongue tickles slowly along my neck. I riffle through my inventory of emotional responses, searching for patience and coming up empty. He wants to explore; I'm ready to explode. Could we be less in sync?

"Off," I order as I tug at his shirt in a desperate bid to regain some control. I pull the soft cotton loose from his jeans and slip my hands inside, letting my fingers skate over warm skin, firm muscle, smooth flanks. The jut of his hip bone feels so right as it fills my palm. "I don't know about you, but most of what I want to do involves you naked. So why are you still dressed?"

That puts the wicked back in his eyes in a hurry, and the shaky hiss of his indrawn breath lets me know he's just as hot for this as I am. Within seconds he's pushed me away, toed off his shoes, and peeled out of his shirt. My mouth goes dry even before his pants hit the floor. His smile says he knows just how he's affecting me. "Better?"

I nod. I know I said before he was good-looking, but now I'm realizing what a major understatement that was. He is sculpted perfection, the most beautiful body I've ever seen bar none. And for right now, it all belongs to me.

Just thinking about it has my dick pushing so hard against the front of my jeans it hurts to draw breath. As for his—it's also hard, longer than I'd expected, though perhaps not as thick around as my own, uncut—something else I wasn't expecting. Rising from a straw-colored thatch of hair, it juts straight at me. Beckoning. My gaze is caught. I swallow hard but still can't force my eyes away.

"Good. Now you," he says even as I'm reaching for him.

I shake my head. "No. Not yet." Call me perverse, but now I'm the one who wants to take my time, to slow down, to explore every inch. Or maybe it's nerves again. Ignoring the surprise reflected in his eyes, I let one hand find his hip again and draw him close. With the other, I fist his cock. He swallows hard, breath rasping in his throat on the exhale. I pump slowly, watching the flush deepen along his chest, his neck. It's so strange touching someone else like this. I want to do more, touch everything, maybe reach down and fondle his sac, but each fresh hitch in his breathing keeps me riveted, keeps my hand gliding up and down his length, unable to stop.

After a moment, he reaches for me, hand on my shoulder, pulling me close. He spears his fingers into my hair once again and draws me in for another kiss. I keep it brief, pulling away again almost immediately. I'm mesmerized by the sight of him. I want to watch his face. I want to see his eyes grow dark, his mouth go slack. I want to hear his breath turn choppy and savage and know it's all because of me.

I rub my thumb across his crown. It comes away sticky and wet, and with that the spell is broken. I can't resist this new lure. I have to taste him.

Taking hold of his arms, I maneuver him around until his back is to the bed. He goes down easy when I push him, bouncing a little as his butt hits the mattress. He leans back on his elbows and grins at me, heat rising up into his cheeks as I kneel between his legs. "You like that, don't you?" he taunts. "Pushing people around, being the one who calls the shots. Did you know I guessed that about you the first time I saw you?"

"Quiet," I order with mock severity. Do I like it? I don't know. I do like this, though. I like gliding my hands over the lightly furred surface of his legs, pressing against them, urging him to spread wider. His balls are nestled in the dusky apex where his thighs meet. I run a finger up along the seam that joins them. They tighten in response. His breath hitches once again. I like that too.

Leaning in, I swirl my tongue around the head of his cock. The flavor is exquisite, familiar yet not, uniquely his. I can't hide the shudder of bliss that rocks through me. I dip lower, run my tongue experimentally over his sac, then gently suck. I'm not expecting the way the scent of him makes my mouth water. I nuzzle the crease where his leg joins his hip, where he's already slick and salty with heat.

My own cock throbs so demandingly I have to stop for a moment and pull back, pressing my hand hard against it, willing it to settle down. Part of me wants to take it out, to strip naked and slide on top of him. I long to rub our cocks together, fist both of them at once, but I don't dare try it. I haven't a prayer of lasting for more than a minute once we're skin to skin, and if I'm going to do this, I want to do it right.

"More," I groan, my voice harsh with need.

It's not a question, but he takes it as one just the same. "Yes," he whispers breathlessly. "Please." He drops his head back and lifts his hips, offering himself to me, and I momentarily lose my breath. He is so insanely beautiful right now. I'm stunned by the sight of him, so open to me. I'm absolutely overwhelmed by how easily he shares himself with me, by the fact he's letting me touch him like this. I can touch him any way I want, so I do.

I open my mouth and take him in, gagging a little at first until I figure out how to relax my throat. There's an instant when his foreskin drags across my teeth and his breath catches, and I worry I might have hurt him, but if there's pain, it doesn't seem to bother him, so I let it go. I need to have all of him, to swallow every last inch; that's all I can focus on, anyway. The smell of his arousal seems to fill the air. I close my eyes to better enjoy the sensations, the way his body shivers beneath my roving hands. I fondle his balls, jostling them gently in their tender sac. I stroke the sensitive space behind them, then slip lower still, fingers trailing along his crease until they're teasing his small puckered hole.

I can't help wondering what would it would be like to push inside, and not just with my finger. To fuck him hard and deep and watch him writhing on my cock. To make him take it all again and again. To erupt within him — and make him take all of that too. Maybe he's right about me. Maybe I do want to be the one in control, or maybe I just want to be the one to make him lose his.

All the while, my mouth is feasting on his dick, head bobbing up and down, alternately sucking and nibbling and swiping my tongue along his length. Words spill from Matteo's lips. At least I think they're words. The thunder of my own heart fills my head, making it hard to hear.

Suddenly, his hand is fisting in my hair, tugging urgently. "Stop. No more now. Please."

I wince at the faint hint of pain in his voice. "Sorry," I mumble as I let him go and climb awkwardly to my feet, embarrassed by my overenthusiastic performance. Obviously, what was not enough for me was entirely too much for him. "I didn't mean to get carried away like that."

"What?" Matteo's eyes widen in alarm. "No, God, don't apologize. Are you kidding? That felt incredible."

"Oh." Relief spreads a smile across my face — probably a real goofy one, at that, but I don't care. "Well, good."

"Yes, it was." Eyes sly in his flushed face, he slides to the edge of the bed. "Very good."

As he moves forward, I take a step back, mostly on instinct, pulling another protest from his lips.

"Oh no, you don't." His hand closes on the waistband of my jeans, and he pulls me forward again until we're practically nose to navel. He grins up at me. "Just where do you think you're going?"

I shake my head. "Nowhere?" I couldn't leave now, not even if he asked me to; my need would keep me welded to his side.

"Damn straight." His eyes smolder. "I didn't stop you because I didn't like what you were doing. I stopped because I don't want to come in your mouth this time."

"Oh. Right." I nod in response, reining in the faint disappointment, because I had wanted that. I'd wanted to feel him exploding on my tongue, filling my mouth with his seed. I wanted to taste him, to tease every last drop from his prick and swallow it down. Then his last words register. *This time.* "I mean... What?" His unspoken assumption that we'll be doing this again makes my head reel. *Yes, please.* That must be what he's saying...right?

Using his grip on me, he levers himself to his feet, takes hold of the hem of my shirt, and begins shoving it upward. "Lift your arms," he instructs, tugging the shirt over my head when I comply. He gets the shirt as far as my elbows; then he stops. With my arms effectively trapped over my head, he leans in and kisses me hard. Now who's the control freak?

Tremors course through me when he presses his naked body against mine, and I can't keep from giving voice to my need and all the unanswered questions in my head. "Matteo." I whimper when his hands smooth down my arms, over my ribs, and back into the waistband of my jeans. No one has ever touched me like this, moved me like this, made me so dizzy with lust and desire. My heart is hammering. As he starts to unfasten my pants, I quickly fumble my shirt the rest of the way off and grab hold of his shoulders, because I know if I don't anchor myself with something solid soon, I'll surely fall down. "Matteo, please..."

"Mattie," he corrects softly, trailing kisses along my jaw as he fondles my erection through the opening of my jeans. "I told you to call me Mattie."

I swallow hard. "Mattie," I reply dutifully. Hell, with his hand wrapped firmly around my cock, I'll call him anything he wants.

"Much better. Thank you." Dipping his head, he bites softly on my shoulder, forcing a groan from my throat. Then he runs his tongue up my neck and whispers, "Now enough with the foreplay. I want you to fuck me."

# Chapter Eight

Mattie's request short-circuits my brain. "What?"

"You heard me. I want you to take this thick cock of yours and bury it in my ass. I want to come with you so deep inside me I can taste you."

His words tear a groan from my throat. Does he know what his words are doing to me? Has he been reading my mind?

"Like that, do you?" he teases. The bad-boy grin on his face tells me yes, he knows exactly what he's doing. Tells me I'm not the only one who gets off on being in control. The throbbing of my cock is damn near painful. At this point, I think I could come humping his leg. I could come just listening to him talk about coming. His voice alone is enough to do it for me. If he keeps this up, I might lose it right here in my jeans.

Who knew being bad could feel this good?

By the time my jeans and boots have joined my shirt on the floor, we're back on the bed, and I'm flushed and heated and quickly approaching meltdown. "Let's see how well we've imagined things," Mattie says, rummaging around in the nightstand drawer, finally pulling out a tube of lubricant. "Mm. Good choice."

He unscrews the cap, squirts some of the gel in my hand and then in his own. I watch as he fingers his ass, preparing himself, getting himself ready — for me — and suddenly, I'm shaking all over once more.

I slick a little of the lube on my cock, but my heart's not really in it. What am I thinking? Maybe it's too much. Or too soon. Perhaps I should just tell him I've changed my mind, that I can't possibly give him what he's asking for. A handjob, a blowjob—they're much more my speed. This, on the other hand—this is kind of huge. It's not the sort of thing you recover from easily or at all. It's not the sort of thing I can chalk up to curiosity, walk away from, and forget.

"Come on, man, hurry up," Mattie urges, nodding toward my crotch. "What're you waiting for? I know I'm not going to last very long, and you look like you could lose it right now."

I open my mouth. No words come out. If we stop now, I think it might destroy me. If we don't stop...that could very well destroy me too.

"Edge?" Mattie's busy hand has stilled. He frowns uncertainly. "Baby, please. I *need* this."

His words and the vulnerability in his tone—so well hidden up until now—startle me out of my self-absorption, make me remember how this whole thing got started. This was supposed to be about Mattie, about healing his issues, his pain, his sense of loss. And here I've been acting as if it was all about me. Have I given even a single thought to his wants and wishes? If I have, I can't recall it.

"Okay." I all but stutter the word. There's something I have to tell him. Something he has to know. "But you might have to help me out a little here. I've never...I've never actually done this before."

"Never done what?" Mattie frowns harder as though trying to decipher exactly what I'm saying.

"This," I say, gesturing clumsily at him, hoping he'll understand without the need for words. "I've never..."

Mattie's eyes widen. "Seriously?"

I nod. "Yes."

"Oh." He gazes at me uncertainly. "Okay... Um, wow, that's...that's not what I was expecting to hear. Do you mind if I ask you why?"

I shake my head. "I don't know. I guess...I just... It didn't ever—" I break off, sighing. "Do we have to talk about this now?"

We stare at each other for another long moment. Please don't stop, I beg silently, perverse as ever. I'm well aware I might have just finally convinced him to change his mind—which is a fine time for me to realize that's the last thing I want. *Please don't say you've changed your mind. Please don't.* I guess it's true what they say. Nothing sharpens a craving quite so much as the threat of loss.

"You do want to, though, don't you?" Mattie asks, his voice cautious, unsteady, reluctant. "'Cause, I mean, if you don't...that-that's okay too."

"No." I shake my head furiously. It's not okay, and there's no way we're stopping now. "That's not what I'm saying. I just... Just give me some guidelines, okay? I don't want to hurt you."

"Is that what's worrying you?" Mattie's smile betrays his relief. "C'mere, baby." Opening his arms, he motions me forward. "Come here and let me take care of you." I crawl between his thighs, and he pulls me to him, hooking one leg around my hip, letting his legs fall open. His foot presses against the small of my back, urging me even closer until our shafts are pressed against each other, trapped between us, leaking precum, pulsing with need. I have to gasp for breath; the animal instinct to grab him and rut, to grind and rub against him till I've shot my load, all but overwhelms me.

Strong hands knead my shoulder, stroke soothingly over my back, calming my impatience. His lips brush mine in a kiss that's clearly meant more to comfort than inflame. "See? That's not too scary, is it? Are you okay with this?"

I nod, even though it strikes me as all wrong—not to mention completely back assward—that he should be the one reassuring me.

"All right, then. We'll just take it nice and slow. Everything will be fine. I promise."

"No." I shake my head, struggling to find the words to explain myself. I won't let him make this about me.

"What?" Dismay grows in his eyes. I see tears form, the first hint of panic take shape.

"This is for you," I say, gazing earnestly at him. "All for you. Gonna make love to you, Mattie. Gonna give you everything I can, whatever you need."

"You *are* what I need," he whispers, the smile returning to his lips, his gaze tremulous. "And I want all of you."

This time when our lips meet, the kiss is searing, hands clutching, bodies thrusting. I reach between us and fist both our cocks—just as I've been longing to do—stroking quickly, getting us both hard and slick and ready. Fluid coats my hand, our shafts, our bellies—I'm glad for it too, since I can't for the life of me remember what he did with the lube.

"Edge, please," Mattie gasps, pushing at me, wrenching his mouth away from mine. "Need you. Now."

I nod. It's time. I give his shaft one final squeeze, then let him go. Levering myself up higher, I slide the tip of my own cock along his crack, seeking his entrance. "Here?"

"Oh yeah," Mattie groans softly in response. "Right there."

I push forward slowly, keeping my eyes trained on his face, gradually working myself inside him. I'm all but blinded by the intensity of his gaze, by the tension in his face and neck and — oh dear God — by the heat, the tightness, the exquisite pressure. It's like nothing I've ever known, like nothing I've even imagined. I'm so deep within him I can no longer tell where I end and he begins.

I move cautiously at first, awkwardly, jerking in fits and starts until I finally find a rhythm. "Yes," Mattie moans when at last I do. He takes hold of his dick and begins to stroke in rapid counterpoint to my own thrusts — hard and fast. His hoarse cries urge me on. "Yes. Fuck, yes. Just like that."

As he'd predicted, neither of us lasts long. In fact, we come together. He explodes in a hot rush that shoots across my stomach, while I let go deep inside him, where the rippling muscles of his ass help to milk my cock dry.

"Heavenly." Mattie sighs as I collapse against him. His fingers comb through the sweat-slickened strands of my hair. "So fucking heavenly. Wasn't it?"

Words are beyond me. I sigh contentedly, expecting to leave it at that until his voice comes again.

"Edge? Everything okay?"

Eyes closed tight, I nod in reply. It's better than okay. It's perfect.

"So…your first time? Really? That… I gotta tell you, babe, that's kind of blowing my mind right now."

It's blowing my mind too. Just remembering is enough to have me craving more — to have me wishing I could have lasted longer, experimented more. Maybe next time. If there is a next time. I exhale at the thought — a shattered sigh muffled by the press of my face against Mattie's neck. *Please God, there has to be a next time.* Even though my capacity for rational thought is less than optimal at the moment, I really can't imagine how anything in creation could possibly feel better than this. I mean, seriously, screw salvation. If I had nothing more to look forward to than an eternity of this, it would be fine by me. But once was definitely not enough.

\* \* \*

"At least tell me I didn't just seduce you against your will," Mattie murmurs a short while later, shocking me out of what had been a pleasant stupor. "Please."

"What's that?" We're still sticky and sweaty and tangled up with each other, arms and legs entwined, both of us too happily sated to move, or so I'd thought. Confused, I open my eyes. He's worrying his lip with his teeth and looking…really quite adorable. I can't help but smile at the sight of him. "What did you just say?"

"This isn't funny," he insists, shoving at me until I let him go. "I've been thinking about what you said, and…and I'm serious. Tell me."

"I would if I understood the question." I settle myself on my side with my head propped on my hand. Seduced? Yes. Definitely. But… "Against my will?"

Mattie nods, looking annoyed and a lot closer to miserable than I'd expected. I feel a little of my own happiness drain away.

"When you said you'd never done this before...you meant with another man, didn't you?"

I feel the flood of heat in my face. What else did he think I meant? Had I really seemed that inexperienced? I don't imagine any man likes to hear that! "Do we really have to talk about this?"

Mattie glares at me, and I don't know why I even bother asking. Of course we have to talk about it — when does he ever not want to talk?

"I knew you were reluctant, but I figured you just needed to be convinced."

"Yeah?" I run what he's just said through my head a couple of times. It seems like a pretty accurate assessment. "So what's your point?"

He sighs impatiently. "I thought we both wanted the same thing, that we were both on the same page, batting for the same team."

I stare at him blankly. I've never been particularly good at deciphering metaphors, even at the best of times. "Come again?"

"Don't you get it? I assumed you were gay."

"Oh." I wince a little at that. He notices, of course. His eyes flash angrily, his lips tighten in displeasure, but I can't help that. A lifetime of secrecy and denial takes a little while to overcome. I'm not comfortable with labels in general, but that one more than most. "Does it make a difference?"

"Edge." Mattie glares at me, clearly exasperated. "Of course it makes a difference. You should have said something if...if that wasn't the case."

"Sorry." Heart sinking, I drop my gaze and look away. Maybe he thinks this was a mistake. Maybe we'd have been better off if I'd trusted my instincts and kept my distance. Kissing him on the beach—that's where I first went wrong. But who am I kidding? I was a goner from the start. Those puppy-dog eyes—they had me from well before we said hello. And mistake or not, I can't regret a minute of it. I just wish I knew he felt the same.

"You should have said something," he repeats stubbornly. "Why didn't you just tell me if you weren't interested?"

Not interested? Startled, I glance back up at him. "What?" There's a hint of anger in Mattie's tone that seems totally out of proportion. How did we get from heavenly to here in no time flat?

"I realize I probably seemed a little pathetic to you, but I wish you would have just leveled with me. I assure you I wasn't looking for a...for a pity fuck."

"Okay, where is this coming from? Of course I was interested—am interested. I-I want you so much I can't stand it. What part of that did I not make clear to you?"

"But you're not gay, right?"

I look away again. I'm hating this discussion. Why do we have to talk about this at all? "I don't know what I am. All right? Why do you have to slap labels on people, anyway?"

"Because it makes communication easier," Mattie snaps. "That's why. And because it prevents this kind of misunderstanding."

Okay, now that makes me mad. "Really? Is that how it seems to you? 'Cause from where I'm sitting…not so much."

"You never had sex with a man before—isn't that what you just told me?"

"So what? I never did a lot of things, Mattie. What's the point? The opportunity never arose."

"Yeah? How come? There were no men where you came from?"

"Let's just drop it." I get out of bed and start searching for my clothes. Arguing naked—there's something else I haven't done before. And I really don't care if I never do it again either. "I'm just not as comfortable as you seem to be about discussing my sex life. All right?"

"Oh sure," Mattie answers. Still naked. Still not bothered about it at all as far as I can tell. And still hell-bent on arguing with me. "Except we just had sex, in case it's escaped your attention."

I close my eyes as the memories flood in, rendering me momentarily breathless. "Believe me, I'm very well aware of the fact." I can still feel him everywhere. There's not an inch of my body that doesn't want to feel him again. Just thinking about it makes me hard—and how stupid is that? Especially when there's not a chance in hell he'd be willing to do anything about that now. If anyone's pathetic here, it's clearly me.

"And since there's been no one else, from what you tell me, I guess that means I am your sex life. And I do want to discuss it."

"Fine. Whatever. Have it your way." I give up the search for my clothes—I'd never be able to get my jeans on now, anyway—and sit back down on the bed. "What is it you want to know?"

"Why you did it, of course. When you said... Oh shit, it's not just the job, is it?"

"The job?"

"Yeah. You know, showing me the ropes? Helping me get settled in? Please tell me that's not all I was to you."

"Oh." I close my eyes again. My face is so hot my ears are burning. "No. Hell no. It's got nothing to do with...with that." We're both naked. We're in bed. We just got through having sex. Now he wants to talk about ropes? Again? My stomach heaves. My chest grows tight. "I swear to God, Mattie, if we don't stop talking about...about things like that, I'm going to be sick here in another minute." I bury my head in my hands and groan. "Just stop, all right? Please? I can't take any more. I don't know what else you want me to tell you."

I feel Mattie's hand on my shoulder as he slides over to sit beside me. "Hey...are you all right?"

"No. Definitely not all right."

"What's wrong? Are you sick? Is there anything I can do for you? Someone I should call?"

I shake my head. Useless to tell him that "sick" is a matter of opinion. I've been called that before. "I don't want to fight with you. That's what's wrong. I don't want to ruin what we have between us." My voice drops to almost a whisper. "What we did...being with you like that...it feels more right than anything I've ever done before. Please don't take that away from me."

"It was good for me too," he answers quietly, adding after a moment, "So...you're saying it's not just something I imagined? This thing between us goes both ways? I didn't just push you into it? You really did want to be with me?"

"Did I want you?" I lift my face and stare helplessly at him. He's so damn beautiful, and I ache with the need to have him under me again—right this minute. Of course I want to be with him. Who wouldn't? "Yes. More than life itself."

Mattie blinks. A blush steals across his face. "Um...okay, but you do remember we're both dead now, don't you?"

"More than anything, then," I say, correcting myself. "All right? And I'd give anything if I could just take back these last couple of minutes and go back to how things were when we...when I was making love to you."

"Oh, Edge." Mattie lays his hand on my thigh. I stare fixedly at it, resisting the urge to move it higher. "I'd like that too."

I place my hand over his, twine our fingers together, feel the tightness in my chest begin to ease. I don't know what it is about this one. I can't explain anything about the way he makes me feel. No wonder he's so frustrated with me. I'm frustrated with myself.

"So that's it, huh?" he asks after a short silence. "After a lifetime of heterosexuality, I turned you gay using nothing but the power of my unbearable hotness?"

I know he's teasing, but there's a wistfulness there too—a need to hear what I can't quite find the words to say—and it tears at my heart. "It's more than that, all right?" I tell him, still struggling for the right words. "You make me feel okay."

"Okay?" Mattie's head snaps back. Red stains

appear on his cheeks. "I'm sorry. Did you just say I make you feel okay? Not great, not incredible, not even good. Just...okay?"

"Stop it," I say, weary and worn down and just this side of giving up. He tries to pull his hand from mine, but I refuse to let him. "Would you fucking stop it? That's not what I meant, all right? Will you just listen for a minute? I mean okay with myself, with who and what I am."

"You mean gay?"

"Why do you have to name it? All I know is that for the first time in as long as I can remember, I'm all right with just being me, with not...pretending to be something or someone I'm not. That's not such a small thing."

"No, I guess it's not, is it?" Mattie smiles at me. "I'm sorry I was such a pain in the ass. I didn't understand. Thank you for explaining it to me."

He leans in to kiss me, and my blood surges with relief. I'm so happy to have him back, to have this back, and suddenly, I realize just how much I left out of my explanation.

"Wait," I say, pulling back, laying my hand against his chest to hold him off. "There's more."

He looks startled. "What do you mean more?"

"How you make me feel, it's more than okay. For the first time ever I'm actually glad for...for the way I am. I'm happy for it. You make me happy, and right now I-I wouldn't want to be any other way but how I am."

"Oh. My. God," Mattie whispers in a voice that's husky and strained. His eyes have gone dark. His cheeks are twice as flushed as before. "That better not just be a line you're handing me."

I shake my head. "It's not. I promise."

"Well then, I guess there's only one thing I can say in response." He frames my face with his hand and smiles—a wicked-beautiful smile that sets my heart to pounding. "You are so getting laid. Right now. Again."

His words—and that look on his face—startle a groan from my lips. Unable to stop myself, I take hold of his shoulders and tumble onto my back, pulling him down with me just like I wanted to do when we were on the beach. The solid weight of him feels so good, his body plastered against mine as I twist around, rolling with him until we're both stretched out on the bed once again. I hook my calves over his legs to keep him close, cradling his hips between my own. We're both right where we belong—I know it.

I lift my face to his. I want to plunder that beautiful mouth once more, to devour it anew, to rediscover and lay claim to every last inch. I'm so intent on my mission, I can only blink in surprise when he draws back, eluding me. "Come here," I order…beg…whatever.

He smiles and shakes his head. "Not this time you don't."

I reach for him anyway, certain he doesn't mean it. Or at least certain that, even if he does, I can change his mind.

"Hey." Still smiling, he grabs my wrists and pins them to the bed. "Am I gonna have to restrain you to get you to behave?"

His words wrap me in darkness. I feel the terror set in, the whispery touch of phantom ropes pulling tight at my neck, my wrists, my groin. And just that quickly, I go blind with panic.

Gulping for breath, I pull free of his hands. I shove him aside and lever myself up on one elbow. My chest is heaving. My heart pounds as I drag my fingers through my hair, then over my face, my throat, my chest. My guts are a mass of quivering knots. I flex my fingers, try to will away the memories. I'm pretty sure it's hopeless, though.

"Edge?" Sitting back on his heels, Mattie watches me, his expression concerned and understandably confused. "What is it? Talk to me. What's wrong?"

I shake my head. Even if I had the words to explain what I'm feeling, I wouldn't give them to him. Some secrets are too destructive, some sins too black to share.

"I just figured it should be my turn now," Mattie explains, his voice as gentle as the hand he lays on my chest, rubbing slow, soothing circles. "You know? I just wanted to be the one to make you feel good."

My brows draw into a frown. What's he talking about now? "You have been making me feel good. You've been doing that all along." It shouldn't need to be said again. He should know how I feel by now. How has he missed seeing what he does to me?

His lips quirk. "No, I'm pretty sure that was you. You're the one who's been doing all the heavy lifting up until this point."

I shake my head again. "Not true." We never would have gotten here if it weren't for him, if he hadn't kept after me, if he hadn't pushed. This has all been him. All of it.

"Just let me have this, okay?"

He leans in close, teasing me with soft kisses against my throat, my chest. The rasp of his beard sends shivers of awareness spreading in waves across my skin. His teeth close briefly on one nipple, shocking another groan from my lips. Hard. I'm so hard. I'm still aching for him—though I don't know how that could possibly be the case. "Mattie—"

"Please. Let me be the one to get us there this time."

"This time?" I repeat the words carefully. He's said them before. I'm still not certain what they mean, but I really need to know.

A soft laugh bursts from his lips. "Yes, this time. That's all I'm asking for right now. I promise you can have your wicked way with me again later—as much as you want, okay?"

As much as I want? I nod, dizzy with the thought. "That could be a lot, you know."

He smiles. "Good. I hope it is. But occasionally you're going to have to let me do things for you too."

"Anything," I say, my voice breathless and hoarse. "Whatever you want."

Mattie's eyes turn smoky. "Careful," he cautions as his gaze slides down over my body. My hips buck as though I'd been touched, but it's from nothing more than the heat in his eyes. I'm impossibly hard now, painfully, excruciatingly, wonderfully hard. "Don't go saying things you don't mean."

I open my mouth, about to protest that I do mean it, when it strikes me that...well, perhaps he has a point.

"Anything—that could cover a lot of territory, you know. Why don't we both just take things slow and see where that leads us, okay?"

"Why're you doing this?"

My question takes both of us by surprise, I think, but suddenly I really want to know. He frowns. "I just told you. I figure it's my turn."

"Yeah, but so what? It sounds like you've had a lot of guys. What makes this so special? Or did you make this much effort with all of them?"

Mattie shrugs. "Not all of them, no."

"So why me?" That puts the teasing smile back on his face. He reaches for me. I hold him off. "Don't try and snow me, Matt. You already made it clear you don't believe in soul mates or love at first sight. We just met, and I'm no one special, so why not just walk away at this point?"

"Is that what you want me to do?'"

I shake my head. "You know that's not what I'm saying. But you're the one who said you didn't want this to be just pity or a job or anything like that. I don't either." I'll still take it, even if that is the case, but at least I want to know what I'm getting myself into.

"Haven't you ever met someone and just had a feeling about them? Like maybe you always knew them—something like that?"

Until now? Not really. I shrug. "I don't know. Maybe. Is that what this is?"

"I don't know what it is," he answers. "I'm as much at sea as you are. But I like you, Edge. Isn't that enough for now?"

"I guess." I nod again and then clear my throat. "So…you said something about making me feel good?"

That smoky gaze ignites. "That I did."

He pushes on my shoulder, and I roll over onto

my back willingly enough, but I brace myself on my forearms, head raised. There's no way I'm going to miss watching his every move.

He starts off slow—feathering kisses along my face and neck—then moves back to my chest.

Strange that I never considered my nipples an erogenous zone before. He teases them now with teeth and fingers, and lightning jolts me. "Fuck, Mattie!"

He glances up, grinning. "Not yet. We'll get to that in a bit."

He shifts lower. My muscles quiver under the stroke of his hands and mouth. His tongue dips into my navel, fingers drifting even lower to tug gently at my sac. My cock jerks in response, begging for attention. He ignores it. His mouth licks the crease of my hip, whirls circles around my sac. He draws first one ball, then the other into his mouth, sucking softly; meanwhile his fingers dance lightly along the seam of my ass, toying dangerously close to the tight little pucker.

I inhale sharply as he shifts to kneel between my legs. My thighs spread wide to accommodate him, laying me open to his gaze, vulnerable to his touch. His. I'm his. A wave of dizziness washes through me, and I have to shut my lips tight to keep from crying out. I want his mouth on my cock so badly. Want to fist my hand in his hair and force him to take me.

What I get instead is the slide of his tongue along the underside of my shaft, and it's not enough. God, not nearly enough. "More, Mattie, please…"

He does it again. And again. Good. So good. But still not enough. I groan each time he pauses to lap up the glistening drops that pearl from my slit—for him, all for him. My toes curl and flex with every stroke of his tongue: down and then up, around the ridge, over the top, down again, up.

My attention follows the trail his tongue takes, breathless, spellbound, shameless for his mouth. I don't even realize when my hips begin rocking; all I know is that I ache for him to take possession of me. I don't even know what I mean by that. I don't even know if I care. My fingers are fisted in the bedclothes, arms trembling with the effort to keep from reaching for him. "Mattie. Now," I beg again.

What I get this time is his lips engulfing the head of my cock, his throat opening to swallow me down. *Finally!* Shock forces a cry from my lips as every nerve in my body broadcasts its pleasure. My balls burn at the speed with which they contract. I drop back my head and practically howl, "Fuck, yes."

From there on in, it's hard and fast. The wet heat of his mouth on my shaft. The pistoning of my hips. The shivery scrape of his nails along my thighs as he tries to hold me down. If he scratches any harder, he'll leave marks. I'm shocked by how much I want that, how the very idea has my hips bucking harder — just to feel his fingers tighten on my flesh.

I'm so lost in the pleasure I have no idea what he's up to. It's not until the climax has caught me up that I realize he hasn't gotten off too. Next time, I think, even as I feel my cock start to pulse, pumping my seed down his throat. Next time it's my turn to do this, to drive him out of his head.

As soon as I recover, I plan on throwing him down and turning the tables, taking his cock in my mouth and giving no quarter, swallowing him until he shoots, until he fills my mouth with his thick, salty flood. I'm dizzy with the thought of it, with the need for it. I'm drunk on it, actually. Drunk on nothing more than the thought of his cum. The idea seems odd, but totally plausible at the moment. Why shouldn't it be possible?

Why shouldn't anything be possible? True love. Salvation. Predestination. Fate. Why shouldn't anything be possible at all?

# Chapter Nine

It's not usual for Lorraine to ask for progress reports, but I don't know why I'm surprised when she does this time. Nothing about this job has been usual—and trust me when I say I'm really not complaining about that. I'd say these have been some of the best days of my life if it weren't for the fact that I'm dead and "day" doesn't really have any literal meaning here. But however you want to look at it and however long it's been—call it days, call it weeks, call it no time at all—I've never been happier. Not even a visit with Lorraine can take that away from me.

"You wanted to see me?" I ask, trying to hide my smirk. Nothing like stating the obvious. We both know I wouldn't be here for any other reason. Ever since our affair went sour, we've both done a bang-up job of keeping out of each other's way.

She gazes at me thoughtfully; I look her over in return. It doesn't take very long. She's a little bit of a thing, after all, maybe five feet two, blonde and curvy, a total babe, and despite everything we've been through, I can't help smiling just a little.

What can I say? You don't have to be an artist to appreciate a work of art. And she is that.

She's seated at her desk—a reproduction Louis XV, something I'm aware of only because she told me that's what it is. Why she'd go to the trouble of reproducing a reproduction is anybody's guess. It seems a tad redundant, if you ask me, but to each his own, and I'm sure she has her reasons.

Lorraine has always struck me as being very much a girlie girl, which is what initially attracted me to her. She reminds me of my wife. Yeah, I was married. Another mistake. Another thing I'll probably never stop regretting. In retrospect, I can see my attraction to them both for what it probably was: a desperate attempt to overcompensate. But that's all water under a very old bridge at this point.

"I was wondering how everything was going?" she asks at last.

Just for an instant, I'm tempted to yank her chain and pretend not to realize she's asking about the job, but the only thing that's going to do is prolong our little chat—and keep me away from Mattie that much longer—so instead I smile and tell her what she needs to know. "Everything's going just fine." If I come across as being a little too pleased with myself, it's only because I am. I'm pleased with myself and amazingly proud of Mattie. He's something of a prodigy, I think. I've never known anyone to pick things up as fast as he does. "Does that surprise you?" I can't help taunting.

Lorraine doesn't answer right away. She's wearing an expression I've never seen on her face before. I think it's uncertainty. Her long pink lacquered nails beat a nervous tattoo against the desktop.

"What?" I ask when the noise begins to grate on my nerves.

"It's just... Well, it's not like you to get so involved—emotionally, I mean. I wonder if the two of you aren't getting a little too comfortable with each other. Maybe losing sight of the objective."

"Comfortable?" I flash on the image of Mattie when I left him, sprawled in our bed yet again. He was wearing nothing but one of those sleepy, sated smiles I've come to know and love so much. Oh yeah, by now

I think it's safe to say we're both as comfortable with each other as it's possible for two people to get. The thought makes me smile and I can't keep from teasing. "What's the matter, sweetheart? Jealous?"

"Don't play games with me," Lorraine warns. Her eyes flash spitefully. "I just wonder if you have any idea what you're doing."

Well that takes a little of the wind out of my sails. I mean, so much for Sophia's theory that I'm good at my job. It's clear Lorraine doesn't share her confidence in my abilities after all.

I could tell her she has nothing to worry about. Like I said, it's been a little while and Mattie's settling in just fine. However, I'm just pissed off enough that I don't want to give her the satisfaction of knowing that. "I guess we'll just have to let the results speak for themselves," I say instead, then I flash her a cocky smile and think myself somewhere else.

\* \* \*

All in all, helping Mattie settle in seems to take no time at all. It wasn't a big surprise when I received notice that I'd been assigned a new task—in fact, I'd been expecting it. What did surprise me, however, was the nature of my new assignments. Being on call to handle emergencies as they come up on Earth was always my favorite, my dream job. The job I never thought I'd be handed again.

I've already been out on several missions now, and I don't think it's possible to be any happier. I finally feel like I'm back where I belong—where I can do some good for someone other than myself. Hell, I'm even willing to admit that perhaps Lorraine wasn't completely wrong in keeping me cloudbound for so long. I was too selfish, too self-involved, too insistent on doing everything my own way—and for my own damn reasons. She was entirely right. I see that now.

I suppose I have Mattie to thank for my change of heart. I never thought I could feel this way about anyone. I lived my whole life without ever having had this. I could feel angry about that—or bitter or cheated or something along those lines—and I know that once upon a time, I would have. But no more. Regret's a nonissue now. I'm just grateful for having finally found it and not about to look this particular gift horse in the mouth.

There is one mystery I still can't decipher, however, and that's the reason behind Lorraine's change of heart. Perhaps she's given up on the idea of tormenting me. Or maybe this is part of some subtle new technique—making me suffer by taking me away from Mattie on a fairly regular basis.

"Or maybe she just doesn't have it in for you as much as you seem to think," Mattie suggests, glancing over his shoulder at me as we share a postcoital shower. His words are almost lost beneath the rush of water. "Did you ever stop to consider you might be a little bit—oh, I don't know—paranoid on the subject?"

I snort in response. "No." Paranoid? Me? Seriously, I want to laugh at the very idea. So I do. Loudly.

Mattie rolls his eyes. "Whatever. Don't stop and think about it for a minute or anything."

"She's evil, baby." I take a break from scrubbing his back, lean in, and kiss his luscious mouth. "Trust me, okay? She's out to get me."

"Well, I liked her. I thought she was nice."

"You what?" I eye him curiously. "What are you talking about? Like her? Nice? When did you two even meet?"

He gazes at me for a moment, his eyes shuttered. Finally he shuts off the water and turns to face me. His hands on my waist, he draws me close. "Promise you won't get mad?"

"Oh shit." My heart sinks. I don't know what's coming next, but I figure no conversation that starts out like that can possibly end well. "What did you do?"

Mattie shrugs. "Not much. I just...talked to her."

"Talked to her?" Man, I'd love to have heard that conversation. Not. The thought has me wincing. My past and present lovers chatting about me, discussing my performance? Yeah, I definitely don't want to know. "What did you say?"

"I thanked her for all her help, and then...I sort of suggested she might want to think about assigning you to do something different for a change."

"You-you did? And that worked?" I'm surprised for all of an instant until I remember how charming he can be, how very difficult to resist. Of course she'd listen to him. Who wouldn't?

"I knew, from what you'd told me, that they'd likely be reassigning you soon. And to be honest, I really didn't like the idea of you...well, you know...teaching someone else the ropes."

It takes me a moment to figure out what he's saying and even longer to realize he's serious. "Baby..." His admission leaves me momentarily speechless. Part of me is loving his possessiveness, the hint of jealousy in his voice, but mostly I'm just amazed—by him, by us. "You know there's no one else for me, don't you?" Mattie can poke fun all he likes at the idea of there being a "special someone" out there for each of us; I know it's true. At least it is for me.

"Yeah, that's right," he murmurs teasingly as I lean in to kiss him. "Make sure you remember that."

"Hey!" I skip the kiss and bite down softly on his lip instead. "That goes both ways, pal. I'm not the one here who's most likely to forget." He's something of a slut, my Mattie. Just one of the many reasons I adore him, if you wanna know.

"Oh?" Mattie's eyes gleam with sudden heat. His expression turns catlike and sly. "So what're you saying, then? Are you gonna punish me if you think it's slipped my mind?"

"Hell yeah, I will." I spin him back around, pushing him until he's facing the wall again. I nip sharply at the juncture where his shoulder meets his neck. "You just see if I don't." I'm still startled by the enormity of my feelings for him, shocked at how completely I've fallen. I cannot believe some of the things he has me doing and saying. Things like this, "You won't be able to sit for a week when I'm done with you."

Mattie, his hands braced on the marble tiles, tilts his hips enticingly. "Mm. Yum." He laughs, obviously delighted by my threat. "I think I may be in need of a reminder right about now." Then he turns serious, and my heart swells when he glances back at me, his gaze gentle. "That wasn't the only reason I talked to her, you know. I knew how much you hated all the babysitting assignments she'd been giving you. You deserve to have something that will make you happy."

But I already have that, don't I? "You make me

happy," I remind him even as I'm reaching for the bath oil. It seems only right to return the favor, to give him what I know will make him happy as well. If this is being unselfish, bring it on.

I nudge his ankles with my foot, urging his legs farther apart. It's more a kick than a nudge, to be accurate. Just sharp enough to sting. Just aggressive enough to elicit that rapturous sigh, that shiver of anticipation I've come to expect from him. I reach between his legs to fondle the heavy sac. A slightly rough, possessive touch—it makes him shudder and moan. The minute I feel him start to respond, however, I stop. This is supposed to be punishment, after all.

After pouring more oil on my hands, I knead his back, taking my time to leisurely measure the span of his shoulders. To lovingly pummel his shower-warmed muscles. To watch the oil bead on his wet skin. Mattie writhes beneath my ministrations. The water has turned his golden hair to bronze. Little rivulets of water sluice down his neck to run the length of his spine. I lean in close, longing to trace their path with my tongue. Impatient now, he pushes his upper body flush against the smooth wall and arches his back until the swell of his ass just grazes my erection.

Electric tingles follow that fleeting contact. With a mock growl, I grab hold of his hips and grind myself against him. "Is this what you want?" I whisper menacingly. With the length of my wet cock wedged firmly between his cheeks, I thrust forward, shaft slipping up and back along his crease.

Mattie's response is a breathy little laugh. "Oh fuck, yeah. Hurry it up, would ya? Put it in already. You're killing me here."

I don't know where this urgency comes from. We've been going at it like rabbits since that first time. You'd think we would have tired of it by now — that at least a little of the novelty would have worn off. You'd think he'd be too sore for this too. But no. We're both as randy as ever. I just can't seem to get enough of him, and I'm endlessly grateful he appears to feel the same.

"Too bad." I push away from him, taking my time to pour more oil on my hands, taking even more time to spread his cheeks and slowly push just the tip of one finger into his ass. "You are just going to have to wait until I'm good and ready to take you. Which may not be for quite some time yet." My voice sounds miles cooler than I'm feeling. I push deeper, watch the digit disappear, knuckle by knuckle, and promptly lose my breath.

What is it about this I find so erotic? Whether it's my cock disappearing into his mouth or my finger into his hole, I never tire of the sight. It never fails to make my heart pound fast, to make my balls draw tight. Despite all my big words, I know I won't last long. There's a tremor in the backs of my thighs, and I haven't even touched myself yet. Good thing too. At this point, I think I'd go off at the first stroke.

"Oh God, Edge." Mattie jerks his hips frantically, forcing my finger to slip even deeper inside him. "Move, damn it. I need it. Now."

"I know you do." I do too, but still I take my time. I want to make this good for him. I want to make it last. I want to draw things out until we're both insane with need. I've mostly gotten over my fear that this time will be the last time — the only time — he'll let me do this to him, but what if I'm wrong? What if this is the last time? What if there isn't any more. "I'm not gonna let you rush me."

Forcing the thoughts away, I pump slowly in and out, first with one finger, then two. He pushes back again and again, impaling himself, forcing me deeper. I love the suctioning heat of his tight passage, the greedy hunger with which his opening expands to accommodate me, as though it would swallow me whole.

An endless string of mostly curses falls from Mattie's lips as he writhes on my finger, pleading with me to give him more, to do it now, to fuck him harder, faster, deeper.

He lifts one hand away from the wall, and I know he's going for his cock, so I grab his wrist with my free hand to stop him. If I can't have it, neither can he.

"Leave it there," I order more than a little breathlessly, forcing his hand back where it was. The slap of his open palm reconnecting with the wet tile is loud and hopelessly erotic—like the crack of a whip. I cover his hand with my own to hold it in place. "Don't move till I tell you."

"God, Edge," Mattie groans in tortured delight. "You're such. A fucking. Tease."

I have to laugh. Just who does he imagine is responsible for that? I lean forward until I have him trapped against the wall. I plunge my tongue into his ear and whisper, "Baby, I'm just getting started."

I'm lying, though. The way we're touching now, skin to skin from practically our knees up to our necks, is utter bliss, but every second spent this way shreds another strip out of my self-control. Within minutes I'm pressing my lips to his ear and whispering urgently, "Need to."

Mattie nods, whimpering softly as I pull my fingers from him. I can't reach for the oil one-handed, but luckily there's more than enough precum dribbling from my slit to do the job. A quick couple of strokes are all it takes to slick my shaft; then I'm plunging inside him.

His body welcomes me, a tight, wicked warmth that feels like home. Our left hands are still clasped together against the wall, but I reach around him with my right to take his shaft in hand. We're locked together, pumping and sliding, bodies struggling for release. He reaches his free hand back to clutch at my thigh. I let my teeth close on his shoulder.

All too soon he's stiffening in my grasp. Icy flames lick down my spine. My balls contract. At the first tightening of his internal muscles around my swollen shaft, I go off like a rocket. Cum spills over my hand, a thick, hot flood, even as I let loose inside him.

We jerk hard against each other, again and again, slowly winding down until all motion has ceased except for the tandem heaving of our chests, the faint aftershocks trembling in our muscles. Mattie's forehead is pressed against the wall. My own face is pressed against his back. Despite the weakness in my legs, the lightness in my head, I think I could happily stay like this forever.

Without looking, Mattie reaches for the faucet. I have less than a second's warning before water is raining down on both our heads. Laughing, I lift my face into the spray, let the water fill my mouth. Then I squirt a stream into his ear.

He chokes back a laugh as well, trying to bat the water away with his hands. Then both of us are reaching for each other at the same time, coming perilously close to losing our footing and landing in a heap on the slippery floor.

I'm still laughing when the internal alarm goes off, telling me I'm needed elsewhere. Groaning, I grab his shoulders. I lean in to brush a quick kiss across his lips, then let him go again.

"Hey, come back here," he protests, reaching to pull me back, but I elude his grasp.

"Sorry, babe," I say as I get out of the shower. I take a towel from the shelf by the door and briskly wipe myself off. "Hold that thought. Gotta go."

"What? Now?" Mattie follows me back into the bedroom, a frown on his face as he watches me dress. "You're kidding me."

"Nope. Duty calls. Earthly emergencies wait on no angel's pleasure."

He falls back on the bed with a groan. "Maybe you were right about Lorraine after all," he mutters, looking adorably frustrated. "Maybe she is trying to get even with you. Or maybe I'm the one she's trying to make suffer."

"More likely she's trying to get me out of the way so she can hit on you herself." I'm joking, but it could very well be true. He's so freaking gorgeous I almost forget I'm in a hurry to leave. "You be good while I'm gone, you hear me? I promise I'll be back as soon as I can."

Mattie sighs fretfully. "I don't get it. Why do you have to go now? I thought time was an illusion?"

"It is. But it's a persistent one." I think it was

Einstein who said that.

* * *

There's an ambulance speeding through the streets of Los Angeles. I'm in the back, offering comfort to the worried young mother. She can't see me, which is the case more often than not. People only see us when we need them to—which is a lot less often than you might think. You'd be surprised at how much we can accomplish without ever making our presence known.

The reason for our reticence is simple. It's the message that's important—not the messenger. I didn't always understand that as well as I do now. In the past, I'd have been more focused on me. On what I was going to do next. On how I was going to handle things.

Tonight I realize it's all about them: the pale redhead with the worried blue eyes and her daughter. The little girl has suffered a seizure brought on by a high fever. She's unconscious now. Her eyes are closed, and her golden lashes lie too still atop her rosy cheeks. I lay a cool, healing hand on her brow to ease her discomfort. I clasp her mother's hand and whisper silently, "It will be okay."

It will *always* be okay, no matter what. That's something else I'm finally realizing. Everything—even this—is part of some perfect divine plan. We just don't always see it for what it is.

And yes, I said we. It's like I keep trying to tell you—none of us is perfect. None of us knows everything. We're all just muddling along, doing the best we can.

As soon as we arrive at the hospital in Santa Monica, the little girl is whisked away. Her mother is occupied for a time with filling out forms and answering questions, but then she's left alone—with a clipboard and a new set of forms. That's when the fear really hits her. That's when I decide to take physical shape. She just needs someone to talk to—a hand to hold, a shoulder to lean on. She just needs to know she's not alone. It's the same thing we all need, really.

Her hands are shaking. From the way her wide eyes stare blankly at the paper, I can tell she's too frightened to even read the questions printed there.

"Would you like some help filling out that paperwork?" I ask as I sit down in the chair beside hers.

Her eyes widen in surprise for an instant, and a wobbly smile appears on her face. I smile back at her reassuringly. What she sees when she looks at me depends in large part on what she wants to see. Tonight, it appears she wants to see me as a young man, tan and fit with light brown hair, dressed in a set of pale blue scrubs with a stethoscope around his/my neck.

"Thank you," she murmurs faintly, still staring at me with a mixture of hope and surprise as I reach out and gently remove the clipboard and pen from her hands.

"You're here with your daughter?" I ask. Her smile fades a little. Her chin quivers as she nods. "Don't be afraid. She's in good hands. She'll be all right."

Tears well up in her eyes. "I want to believe that. I do. But this place…" I watch as she gazes around helplessly. "I-I can't…I can't stand it here. I can't…"

Her fear is palpable. It puzzles me. The waiting room is quiet and relatively empty, hardly a panic-inducing environment. "What is it you're so afraid of?" I ask, but before she can answer the door to the parking lot slides open and another worried-looking young woman rushes in.

The newcomer glances around frantically, relaxing only a little when she spies the woman beside me. "Meg!" she calls as she hurries toward us. "Where is she? What happened?"

The woman beside me scrambles to her feet. "Oh, Beth!" she wails as she launches herself into the other woman's arms.

I stare at the women as they hug, alternately crying and comforting one another. I'm amazed and startled by what has to be a coincidence. Meg? Beth? How weird is that? I mean, seriously, what are the odds?

But there's something I'm forgetting about coincidences, and it's this: coincidences are an angel's stock-in-trade. They're our calling cards, if you will. They exist purely because we've rearranged the necessary circumstances in order to create them. They're little more than a wink, wink, nudge, nudge from the celestial realms.

I glance again at the forms attached to the clipboard in my hand and notice, for the first time, the name scrawled at the top of the page: *Megan O'Connell*.

Apparently, today the odds are really good.

# Chapter Ten

"I can't lose her, Beth." Meg sobs while Beth does her best to calm her. "Not her too. Not both of them. I can't bear it. I can't."

"I know," Beth murmurs as she strokes Meg's hair. "Sweetheart, I know. We won't. I can't either."

*That's Meg. Mattie's Meg.* Suddenly, I'm wondering what I've really been sent here to accomplish.

Mattie and I have tried several times without success to return to the Hall of Records. I'm still locked out, and it appears his desire to learn more about the daughter he may or may not have fathered has been judged as nonessential.

I'm not sure who's responsible for making all these decisions, but whoever they are, they're wrong. Dead wrong. I know it would make a difference to him if he knew the truth. Even if the answer is not the one he wants to hear, it would still help him find closure. That might not be my assignment anymore, but I don't care. I have an opportunity here to help him, and I'm not going to let it pass me by.

I get to my feet and approach the women. "Excuse me," I say as I gently pry them apart. I hand Meg back the clipboard and pen. "Why don't you get started with these, and I'll be right with you."

Then I turn to Beth and smile reassuringly. "I just need to ask your girlfriend some questions about her daughter. Maybe you could go find the cafeteria and get her a cup of coffee or something? I'm sure she'd appreciate that."

"My *wife*," Beth snaps, "doesn't drink coffee."

"Well, all right, how about some tea, then?" I suggest right before it hits me. "Wife?" And again I'm thrown off balance. Mattie had referred to them as partners. Is this more news I can share with him? Damn, but I'm on a roll today. "Well, all right. Good for you. Congratulations. Way to go."

Beth glares at me. "Who are you? What the hell's going on?"

"Look," I say as I draw her a little farther away. "I know you're upset, but Meg is too. One of you has to be strong here, and I'm thinking that's you."

"S-st-strong?" Beth's face turns chalky. She clutches at my arm. "Oh my God. What are you saying? What's happening? Where's my daughter?"

"Everything's fine," I promise. "Everything's just as it should be. Just give us a few minutes. All right?"

* * *

"Why don't you tell me about your little girl," I say as, once again, I sit beside Meg and take the clipboard from her hands. "Has she ever had this kind of reaction before?"

She shakes her head no. Her lip is quivering, and tears are welling up in her eyes. I know it's only a matter of time before she loses control, but I can't keep from pushing her for information. "And what about you? Any family history of this sort of thing?"

"I don't know." Meg's brow furrows as she tries to think. "I don't think so. Not that I remember."

"Okay. How about her father, then?" It's the million-dollar question. I hold my breath while I wait for her answer.

Meg shakes her head. "No. I don't...I don't

know. He-he's dead." A sob breaks from her throat, and the tears begin to fall in earnest now. "I'm sorry. I-I can't talk about this anymore."

"I understand." I lay the clipboard aside and wait, knowing full well that she can't not talk about it either. "This is where it happened, isn't it? That's why being here makes you so upset?"

She nods and tries to brush away the tears. I materialize a tissue and hand it to her. "Thank you," she whispers as she dabs at her face. "I can't believe he's gone, you know? He was my best friend, and I...I miss him so much. I just wish he was here."

"I'm sure he misses you too," I murmur soothingly. "I know he'd be here with you if he could — with you and his little girl."

"He never even knew about the baby." Meg sighs woefully. "Isn't that awful? He died not knowing. And it was all my fault. It's my fault he's dead."

"No, it's not." I shake my head. "Don't be silly. How was it your fault? It was an accident. It wasn't anyone's fault."

Meg frowns. She stops sniffling long enough to shoot me a startled look. "How did you know it was an accident?"

"What? Oh. I...uh...I guess I just assumed. Was I wrong?"

"No. It *was* an accident. He was killed by a car. But it was still my fault. He was buying me a present when he died. He was trying to cheer me up. I'd been upset, worried — and all over nothing! I was so stupid! If only I'd —"

"Stop it." I clasp her hands in mine like I did in the ambulance. "He'd hate it if he knew you were blaming yourself. I know he would. And besides, you can't know what would or wouldn't have made a difference. Maybe it was just his time and there was nothing anyone could have done to change that."

Meg shakes her head. "No. That's not true. He didn't have to die. He could have gotten out of the way. He could have saved himself. But he didn't. And...I know it's awful...but I'm just so angry at him I want to scream."

I smile at her. "So now it's his fault? Come on, Meg, you don't believe that either. Sometimes things happen so fast there's no time to react. People freeze. They don't know what to do. I'm sure if he could have gotten out of the way, he would have."

But I don't think she's even listening to me. "It was just so like him, you know? He was always so thoughtful, so kind. I told him all the time he had a savior complex. He always had to be helping people, you know?"

I nod doubtfully. That sounds like my Mattie, all right, but where's all this anger coming from? "You say that like it's a bad thing."

"Well, maybe it is." Lifting her chin, she meets my gaze. Her eyes are full of hurt and rage and challenge. "He could have been here with me now — with me and my little girl. Our little girl. But he's not. He's not. He chose to die instead. He just had to be a hero."

"A hero?" I try to keep the skepticism out of my voice, but I'm not sure I succeed completely. Since when does being hit by a car make someone a hero? I mean, sure, I understand the human need to glorify the dearly departed, really I do. But let's keep things within reason, people. It's sad and tragic when someone dies so young, but there's more to being a hero than merely dying violently.

"He could have saved himself. He could have jumped out of the way. It was the shopkeeper who froze—not him. She was so scared she couldn't move." Tears have begun streaming down Meg's face. She slips her hands free of mine and swipes uselessly at her face with the now-sodden tissue. I hand her another.

"She came to his funeral. That's how we found out. She brought the present he'd been buying…to give to me. She said she didn't know who it was for, but she figured I'd be there. That's when she told us what happened. How Mattie pulled her out from behind the counter and shoved her out of the way of the car. That's why…" Meg draws a deep, shuddering breath and dissolves in tears again. "That's why he's dead, and my little girl is all I have left of him. And if she dies…I'll have no one, nothing. I'll be all alone."

"You'll still have Beth," I remind her, absently patting her hand. Beth seems like an okay sort, especially if you've a weakness for churlish and strident. Admittedly, that's not my cup of tea, no pun intended, but Beth sure isn't Mattie.

Even though Meg's loss is—quite literally—my gain, I feel for her. I'm sure there's more I could be doing for her, probably should be doing for her, but I'm too poleaxed by the news she's just given me to really think about anything else.

Mattie's death wasn't nearly as senseless as he'd led me to believe. He died saving someone's life. Un-freaking-believable. Why had he left that part out when he told me the story? Maybe he didn't remember all the details. Maybe he didn't think they mattered. Or maybe he realized it would make me wonder exactly what I can't stop wondering now that I know the truth. Why would someone like him—someone selfless and brave, a hero who'd made his death count for something—ever want to become involved with someone like me?

Luckily, before I have to think about that too hard, the doctor returns.

"How is she?" Meg asks, almost tripping over her own feet in her hurry to stand. "How's Mattie? Can I see her?"

"She's doing much better," the doctor assures her. "And you can see her in a little while. She's sleeping now, so I think we should let her rest. Her temperature's down, and we've started her on antibiotics. We're going to keep her here overnight just to be on the safe side, but I'm sure you'll be able to take her home in the morning."

Meg breathes a sigh of relief. Her shoulders sag, and just as she's wiping her face with the tissue I've given her, Beth returns. I see her out of the corner of my eye. She freezes as she catches sight of us—as she catches sight of Meg, weeping.

"Take deep breaths," I order as I hurry to Beth's side, catching hold of the tea before she drops it. "Everything's okay." I slip an arm around her waist to support her. "Do you need to put your head between your legs or something?"

"Are you insane?" she snaps, shooting me a dirty look. "Let go of me." She makes an unsuccessful grab for the tea, but I lift it out of reach. "Give that back! What do you think you're doing? I'm not going to pass out or anything, if that's what you're afraid of."

Pass out? Now that she's mentioned it, I'm thinking it would be an excellent idea if she did just that. We angels do have some small talents, you know. Putting people into trances and imparting visions are just two of them.

The next thing anyone knows, Beth's eyes roll back, and she slumps against me. I hand the tea off to a startled Meg and lift Beth in my arms.

"What happened?" Meg asks worriedly. "Beth?"

"It's just the shock," I murmur reassuringly as I settle her on one of the chairs. "She saw you crying and feared the worst."

Meg settles herself in the chair next to Beth's, biting her lip and whispering nervously, "Beth, honey, can you hear me? Please wake up. I'm so sorry I worried you. Please..."

I crouch in front of them and press my hand against Beth's forehead. Before I allow her to return to consciousness, I give her a vision of Mattie. I really sell it too. I show her a picture of him, smiling and waving, surrounded by sparkly white and gold clouds. I give him fluffy white wings and a short white robe and a pair of golden gladiator sandals. I even put a glittery gold lyre in his hand.

"Oh, man, that's so weird," Beth mutters as her eyes flicker open. She glances around. "What happened? Did I...faint?"

"Here." Meg presses the cup of tea into Beth's hand. "I think you need this more than I do."

Beth clutches at her. "How's Mattie?"

"The doctor says she's doing better," Meg tells her. "She's sleeping, so we can't see her now. But never mind her for a minute. How are you? You scared the shit out of me, fainting like that—are you sure *you're* all right?"

Beth nods. "I think so, but dude, I had a vision. I saw Mattie. *Your* Mattie. You know, Matteo? He's a freakin' angel!"

"An angel?" Meg repeats in disbelief. "You mean like...like what? With wings and stuff?"

Beth nods. "Yeah. Do you believe it? I mean, I saw him up in heaven, right? He was wearing a...wearing a *dress*, or I dunno. I guess maybe it coulda been some kinda toga or something. And...and he was playing a harp."

"Lyre," I correct, suppressing a sigh. I'm not even touching the dress-maybe-toga confusion. Beth is clearly not a respecter of tradition.

"Shut *up!*" Beth snaps at me again. "I am *not* lying."

I shake my head. "Not what I meant. The instrument you saw—it's a lyre, not a harp."

"How do you know what it was?" Meg asks, coming to her wife's defense. "It was her vision, and if she says it was a harp, it was a harp."

Great. Now they're both bristling at me. "Angels play lyres. Not harps. But it's a common mistake. People make it all the time."

"Whatever." Beth rolls her eyes. "I know what I saw, okay?"

I shrug. "If that's true—and it really was a vision—why don't you tell her what he said?"

Her eyes narrow. "What makes you think he said anything?"

"Because that's one of the main differences between a vision and a hallucination. Sometimes it's the only sure way to tell one from the other. Visions always come with a message—otherwise there'd be no point to them."

Meg's jaw clenches. "Look, don't we have more important things to think about—like our little girl, for instance? If Beth says it was a vision—"

"No, Meg, he's right." Beth lays a hand on Meg's arm. "There was a message. And it was for you."

"Really?" Meg asks, her eyes suddenly wary.

"He wanted you to know he's okay—that he's in heaven and he's happy and that you shouldn't be sad anymore. He said maybe this was how it had to be, so that we—you and me and the baby—could be a family. He said you should always remember that he's up there watching over you, over us, until we can all be together again."

"Oh, Mattie." Meg sighs. She doesn't sound angry or lost anymore, merely tired and sad as she sags against Beth's shoulder.

Beth wraps her arms around her. "We'll be okay, babe," she whispers against Meg's hair.

I watch the women hold each other, and I smile. I'm pretty sure my mission here is accomplished. "You ladies be good," I murmur as I get to my feet. I doubt they hear me though. As focused as they are on each other, they don't even notice when I phase out of sight.

Now, I know you're probably thinking I wasn't playing fair, letting them believe Mattie's already in heaven and watching over them. But that's just splitting hairs. Once I get back and tell him what I've found out, I just know Mattie'll be knockin' on those pearly gates in no time flat.

# Chapter Eleven

Lorraine is waiting for me when I get back. She's tapping one patent leather-clad foot impatiently against the granite floor of what looks to be a very large deserted train station and scowling to beat the band. "Just what do you think you're doing?" she demands to know as soon as I come into view.

"Hello to you too," I say, eyes widening as my gaze shifts from our surroundings to her appearance. I gotta say the outfit is a bit of a surprise. Lorraine's usual attire tends toward the frilly and pink. Right now she's wearing a gray tailored suit and a pair of black-rimmed glasses. I guess that's supposed to signify that she means business. Trouble is the glasses are kind of sexy. That and the pouting red lips really undermine the message.

"Is something wrong?" I ask innocently just to watch her temper flare.

"You are unbelievable. Do you know that?"

I'm well aware she doesn't mean it as a compliment, but I can't help playing around just a little bit more. "Thanks for noticing, babe. Now if that's all you wanted to say to me..."

"No, that's not all!" Her hands are fisted on her hips, and she's so clearly angry I'm almost surprised her blonde updo hasn't ignited yet. "I should have known it was a mistake to let you go back to Earth. One routine mission of mercy, but you just couldn't handle it, could you?"

"What're you upset about, Lorraine? I handled things just fine."

"Fine? You call that fine?"

I nod. "Yeah, actually. I do. Where's the problem? I took care of the little girl's fever, made sure there was no long-term damage—"

"What about her mother? You were supposed to comfort her as well, you know, to ease her fears, to keep her from falling into despair."

"All of which I did. In fact, now that I think about it, I handled that assignment better than fine. It was genius what I did there. I took care of her fear and her grief, and I'm pretty sure I helped save her marriage too." I don't know Beth all that well, but I don't think she's done anything to deserve Meg's "I'm all alone in the world" routine. That's the kind of thing that can only breed resentment. And there ain't nothing that'll kill a relationship faster than that.

"Yes, but who asked you to? Who told you to improvise? Why can't you simply follow orders?"

"It's called initiative." Truth be told, her attitude is really starting to annoy me. If she'd wanted someone mindless and uninvolved on this one, she should have sent someone else.

"Initiative?" Lorraine's voice goes up by about an octave—maybe more. "Edge, you knocked that woman out! Just to satisfy your own selfish needs. Just so you could play head games and mess around with things that don't concern you. Don't you ever learn?"

I can't help but roll my eyes at her description. "Could you keep the hysteria in check? It was a perfectly respectable trance, not date rape. Besides, it does too concern me. I wanted to help Mattie find closure. You had to know that'd be the case. I mean, why'd you send me to take care of his kid and her mother if you didn't want me to do what I could to help him too?"

Lorraine's foot starts tapping again, and I find my thoughts derailing. I can't take my eyes off those damned spiked heels. I can't stop thinking about how freaking sexy they look. I have kind of a thing for toe cleavage. I have kind of a thing for this whole corporate-dominatrix look she's got going on as well. Yeah, that part surprises me too, if you must know, but there it is. Now all I can think about is getting back to Mattie. I want to talk him into dressing up. I'm in the mood to do a little role-playing. Those glasses are a must.

I blame him for this too, by the way. Mattie the Corrupter of Angelic Morals. I swear I never had any of these kinds of thoughts before I met him. Or at least not very often. And I certainly never would have acted on them. Much.

The sudden silence makes me realize Lorraine's stopped talking. And I haven't heard a word she's said. She's gazing at me expectantly. I'm starting to get a little tired of that. "What?" I ask with exaggerated patience.

"I said, did it never occur to you that by interfering like this you might be robbing Mattie of the opportunity to accomplish everything he's come here to do?"

"Like what?" I scoff. "The guy's practically perfect. He's a hero, for heaven's sake. He probably shouldn't even be here. What more could he need to do?"

"I guess we'll never know," Lorraine answers in a voice like sweet poison. "Thanks to you, he'll likely be gone before any of us ever get the chance to find out."

"Mattie...gone?" There's an uncomfortable buzzing in my ears. My chest feels tight. I'm having a little trouble with the simple things like forming words and breathing. "What're you talking about? Where's he going?"

Her eyes widen a fraction in surprise. Until this moment I never knew you could combine sympathy and satisfaction in the same smug smile. "Well, where do you think he's going, Edge? Where else would he go once his issues have all been dealt with? He's going to heaven. Where he belongs."

Oh. Right. "Yeah, I knew that." My voice sounds faint and unconvincing even to my own ears. "I mean, that's been the plan all along. Right?" The sad thing is that really is true. That had been my plan. Didn't I say I was going to make it my mission to see he got into heaven as quickly as possible? I guess somewhere along the line I lost sight of the fact that sending Mattie to heaven would also mean telling him good-bye...which leaves me where?

Lorraine is watching me. The look in her eyes is one of triumph...or possibly contempt. It's a little hard to tell. I gaze back at her, considering what my next move should be. The noise in my head is deafening as all my hopes and dreams come tumbling to the ground. The thought of losing Mattie chills me through and through, but I have to face facts. The question now isn't if I'll lose him, but when.

* * *

Obviously, I need a little time before I can face Mattie. So now I'm back on my same old beach. Sitting on my same old log. Staring out at the same old waves.

And thinking my same old sorry thoughts. Or at any rate, similar sorry thoughts.

I can't believe I've gone and screwed up the best thing that's ever happened to me. Or almost screwed it up. I haven't actually done anything too irrevocable yet—assuming Lorraine can be trusted to keep her mouth shut.

That little fact is the only thing keeping me sane at the moment. As of right now, there's still a chance. I could still pull this mess out of the fire.

When you come right down to it, I don't really have to tell Mattie any of what I've learned. And if I don't, he'll probably never even know. You know what they say. Ignorance is bliss. And what you don't know can't hurt you. Only, in this case, it's Mattie's ignorance that may very well turn out to be my bliss, and what he doesn't know...maybe that won't hurt me.

Selfish? Sure. Oh, like that's a surprise, right? But for all I know I could very well be doing Mattie a favor by keeping him in the dark. I mean, what do I really know about heaven? Maybe it's not better. Maybe it doesn't even exist. Maybe we all just get recycled back to Earth instead. Maybe limbo is paradise, and the joke is on the poor suckers who get talked into leaving.

Besides, it's not like Mattie's unhappy with the way things are. It's not like I don't intend to do everything I possibly can to keep him that way. He could stay here. With me. Forever. And never even know the difference, never even realize what he's missing.

But I will. And therein lies the problem.

This place—limbo—it means borderland. The

ancients believed it existed on the outskirts of hell. Personally, I always thought they'd got that wrong. I figured it for the edge of heaven instead. Right now I'm kind of rethinking my stand on the subject.

The never-never land might not actually be heaven, but it sure isn't the other place either. But if I have to spend an eternity staring into Mattie's trusting brown eyes, knowing all the while that I've betrayed him and don't deserve his trust...I guess I might just as well be in hell after all.

In the end, I find I don't have nearly as much of a choice as I'd hoped.

# Chapter Twelve

"There you are." Mattie's eyes light up when he sees me. "You're back."

He's still in our room, right where I left him, making me wonder again about the passage of time here. To me, it feels like I've been gone for most of a day, maybe longer. Did it seem that long to him too? And has he been lying here, sprawled naked across the bed — waiting for me — all the while? Or does it seem to him that only minutes have passed?

I hope it's the latter, and I hope that when he's gone and I'm all alone, I'll still be able to find my way here if I want to and that the days will feel like minutes and the years will feel like days.

Not that it will matter, I suppose. Because they'll all add up eventually — empty and endless — and the weight will surely crush me.

I throw off my clothes as I cross the room. By the time I reach the bed, I'm naked. I drop down beside Mattie and pull him close, then swing a leg over his hips, pinning him beneath me. I slant my mouth over his and kiss him hard, touching him everywhere my hands can reach.

"Eager, are we?" He laughs when I let him up for air. His eyes dance with delight, the joy in them breaking my heart a little more.

"Want you," I growl as I pull him back for more.

"Baby, slow down." He holds me off, his smile turning curious as he combs his fingers through my hair. "What's the rush?"

His eyes are asking a different question, one I do not intend to answer at this point. He's going to be gone soon enough, no sense in hurrying the moment along. I lean in to claim his lips again. "Don't want to talk about it."

Not surprisingly, he does. Worry seeps in to replace the curiosity. "Edge, what's this all about? What's wrong? Did something happen on your assignment?"

"*Really* don't want to talk about it."

"Edge—"

"Call me Michael." The words are out before I realize what I'm going to say, but once they are, I can't say I'm too surprised. Eternity is a really long time. Exactly how long, no one knows. But on the off chance Mattie is ever inclined to interrupt all the heavenly bliss he'll soon be enjoying to think longingly of me, I'd like for him to know just who it is he's missing.

A frown creases his forehead. "All right," he answers slowly. "Michael it is. And who shall we pretend I am?"

"Who said anything about pretending? You asked me once what the rest of my name was, didn't you? Well, now you know."

Mattie's lips twitch. "So let me see if I understand this correctly. You're saying...*you're* the angel Michael?"

At the disbelief tingeing his voice, what's left of my self-control dissolves. I pull away from him and sit up, scowling furiously. "See? This is exactly the kind of crap I was trying to avoid. No, damn it, I'm not *the* angel Michael. I'm *an* angel Michael. *The* Michael is someone else altogether. You got that?"

"Okay. All right. Don't get your wings in a tangle. It's just... You're telling me this now because...

Why, exactly?"

I sigh in defeat. "You're right. It was a stupid idea. Forget I mentioned it." If I start talking now, it will all come out and then...then it will all be over. I need a little more time before that happens. I need a little more of everything before that happens. I'm so fucking needy...it's making me sick. "How about we just don't talk at all?" And not thinking—yeah, that'd be even better.

Mattie flashes me an amused smile. "Whatever you say, Mike." He's chuckling as he twists around and reaches for the lube. "But I gotta tell you, babe, I would have bet anything your name was Dick—just based on how much you seem to like it."

He slicks the glistening gel over his fingers, but before he can get started greasing himself up anywhere else, I stop him. His words have reminded me of something we haven't done yet. Something I'm still not altogether certain I even want to try, except that deep down I know I do. I mean to have everything from him before he goes, and there's no other time but now.

He looks at me questioningly. I gaze back at him, dry mouthed and stupidly speechless. Asking for what I want is proving a lot harder than I'd expected. Could be I'm making a terrible mistake. It wouldn't be the first time. It's entirely possible I could hate this, that it will end up ruining things for both of us. On the other hand, it might be wonderful—which I think would be even worse. Won't that just give me one more thing to regret and miss and long for? Won't that just make eternity feel even more like...well, an eternity?

Either way I'm screwed, I suppose, because I have to know. Call me a masochist, but when I let him go, I want to know exactly what it is I'm giving up.

"Edge?" Mattie asks uncertainly. "Babe, what is it? What do you want? Talk to me."

I open my mouth to tell him, but the words still won't come. Instead I reach for him and pull him close, then drop kisses in the juncture where his neck meets his shoulder. "Can't you guess?" I ask at last.

He doesn't answer right away. He has my head cradled in one hand while his other hand eases slowly down my spine, until his fingers are just teasing the crack of my ass. I shudder in response and tighten my hold on him.

"Edge?" he whispers as his fingers continue their gentle caress, dipping lower, brushing over the sensitive opening, growing bolder with every pass. Rubbing. Circling. Coming back for more. "Edge, love?" His voice is soft, tentative, surprisingly hesitant as he presses one finger inside me.

I swallow hard. "Please," I whisper, barely breathing. "Oh God, Mattie, please..."

I need him to understand what I can't put into words. And he does. I can tell by the tender kiss he presses against my head, by the quiet note of confidence in his voice as he hugs me tight and murmurs, "Okay, babe, okay."

I nod, relaxing a little because I know he means it. Because I know he'll do everything he can to take care of me. Because this is Mattie, and I want everything he's got to give me even if it breaks my heart in the process, which I'm pretty sure it will.

There's a strange sort of freedom in that, I guess. Knowing how this has to end only makes me realize I have nothing more to lose. So why not enjoy what I can of what's left of the ride?

Mattie pulls away. There's an odd expression on his face. He looks pleased. No, he looks proud, like he knows he has me.

And he does. I feel that with every fiber of my being. I'm his. He can have me any way he wants me. I only wish it could be for longer.

He urges me onto my side and then reaches again for the lube. I watch as he squirts out a good amount of gel and try not to hyperventilate when he tosses the tube aside and lies down beside me, his head toward my feet. He slips his hands between my thighs, spreading them wider, wedging his shoulders between them. Slick fingers slide along my crack again, featherlight touches, just skimming my hole—and even so, I tighten in reaction.

"Relax," Mattie whispers, and since he's stroking my shaft with his other hand, teasing my sac with his lips and tongue and teeth...I almost can. "We'll take it nice and easy," he promises. "I'll be careful. I'll go as slowly as you need me to."

I'm thinking that might be forever.

Needing something to do with my hands and mouth, I take hold of his dick. I think I'm just hoping to further distract myself from what's happening down south. I want it. Of course I want it. But on the other hand, if we could have had more time together, if I didn't know it was all ending soon...I know damn well we wouldn't be doing this just yet.

I wrap my lips around the tip of Mattie's cock. He's rock solid and leaking precum, and for some reason that calms my nerves. Being face-to-face with the evidence of how much he wants me is, apparently, just what I need to refocus my thoughts on him.

How can I refuse him what he so clearly wants? How can I not want it for him—no matter what it is?

I let my mouth move steadily over his shaft and try not to wince when he slips a finger inside me. It's a little uncomfortable at first—nothing I can't handle, but nothing I'd go out of my way to look for either. There's a breathless moment or two when he adds a second finger alongside the first, and I can't keep from groaning just a little.

He stills immediately. "Too much?"

There's a shakiness to his voice, a breathless note I've heard there before. He's getting off on this. Fucking my ass with his fingers is turning him on...and I know just how he feels.

"Edge?"

I shake my head. "It's fine. Don't stop." I'm not going to spoil this for him. I'm going to see this through no matter what, let him use me however he wants. "Oh God, Mattie. Want you." How I'll ever survive losing him—that's what I can't imagine.

"I want you too," he says nipping softly on my inner thigh, the sharp sting of his teeth momentarily distracting me from the deeper burn of his fingers twisting in my ass. "C'mon, babe, relax. Just breathe. It'll feel so much better if you do—I promise."

I gasp for breath, struggling to keep things light. "Well, you know, I'm trying to relax, but it feels like someone's gone and stuck a pole up my ass."

Mattie laughs—just as I'd intended. "A pole, huh?" He pumps and stretches me some more. "If you think that now, just wait till we get to the next step."

"Can't wait," I lie, trying for a lascivious grin.

Then I close my eyes, suck on his cock, and try not to think, which is how I almost come to miss it when the sensations gradually change from not too bad to vaguely pleasurable to don't stop gotta have it, at which stage I can't keep from moaning softly. "Mattie..."

He pauses once again. "Still okay?"

I nod. It's better than okay, and I bet he knows it too. I lick harder, tongue rasping over his cock's shiny red crown, so unimaginably soft and slick. So ready to fuck me. I shudder at the thought.

His legs have started to shake. His breath comes faster. It's all he can do to get the words out. "Want more?"

My stomach flutters in response. I can't decide if the answer is yes or no. Instead of answering, I tongue his cock again, tugging gently on the extra skin with my teeth. Maybe he'll make the decision for me.

Mattie moans again, hips bucking. "Edge..."

There's a hint of desperation in his voice now and a question there as well. I'm pretty sure I know what it is he's asking, pretty sure he's not going to make the next move until I give him some sign. And hell, why not? We're both so hard at this point we could probably knock each other out using just our dicks as clubs. It's now or never, I guess. Heart pounding, I surrender and whisper softly, "Yes."

Mattie swipes his tongue around my sac one last time, then shifts away. Even with all the attention he's been giving me, I still go semisoft the instant he sits up, even before he presses on my shoulder, rolling and maneuvering me until I'm facedown on the bed with my knees tucked under me and my ass in the air.

My heart is hammering wildly as he kneels behind me, but at least in this position I can reach beneath me to stroke my shaft. I need that—especially when I feel his hands on my cheeks, spreading them apart. I feel vulnerable, exposed. Then he bends in and teases me with his mouth, tongue spearing into the space he's just opened up, and it's all I can do to keep from crying out. It feels that good.

I groan something incoherent. Even I can't tell what it is I'm saying. Could be I'm speaking in tongues. It's been known to happen. And just like that I'm hard again, ready and wanton, hips rocking in time to the stroke of his tongue.

I pull frantically on my cock, loving the sensations he's giving me, not even caring about what comes next, not even worrying when I spy him going once more for the lube. But then he's positioning himself, aligning the tip of his dick with my entrance, and I'm sucking in air, muscles tensing all over again. "Mattie—"

"Relax, babe," he murmurs, draping himself over my back, hugging me from behind, feathering kisses along my spine. "We'll be okay. Trust me."

I do trust him. That's never been the issue. But then he's lining the tip of his cock up with my ass and urging me to breathe—as if any amount of breathing could erase the thought of what's going on behind me. Between the burn and the sting and the protests of my muscles, I can't remember what the issue is. I try to relax, but that's damned hard to do, and when he straightens up and pulls completely out again, I'm embarrassed at having failed him, but more than a little relieved as well.

"Sorry," I murmur.

"Shh." He pauses for a moment to rub with his thumbs over and around my tight hole, then pushes into me again. A little farther this time. And then back out. I grit my teeth. It's bearable, but not much fun. I try and remember how it felt when our positions were reversed—the mind-boggling tightness, the encompassing heat...

I want to give him that. I do. I want to be that for him. "Just do it," I urge, hoping he'll take the hint.

"Give it a minute," he answers, his voice so tight and breathless and hot my cock jerks in response.

"God, Mattie, please."

"Easy. Relax." The third time... I won't say the head of his cock slides effortlessly past the tight ring of muscle, but it is noticeably easier. He thrusts a little deeper—he's more than halfway home now. My body feels looser, softer. This time when he pulls out, I groan in actual protest. Could I really be craving this? Could I possibly be aching for more? It's unbelievable, but I think I am. It's like an itch that needs scratching or a sore tooth your tongue can't leave alone. Hidden within the pain is the sharp edge of a pleasure unlike anything I've ever known.

"More," I growl hoarsely. "Give me more." So he does. Seating himself fully on his next hard thrust, he brushes against something inside me that startles a cry from my lips. "Yes. God, yes. Do that again."

I shove my hips back, rocking against his groin, trying to force him deeper. That's all it takes. With a shattered cry, he starts pumping into me. Faster and harder with every stroke.

I'm canting my hips higher, rocking back harder,

hungry to take more and more and more. I want it all. The burn and the stretch and the fullness, every glorious, throbbing inch, over and over and over again. "Fuck, yes."

My climax overtakes me so quickly I'm jolted by surprise. I shoot all over the bedcovers, bathing my abdomen and chest in luscious, sticky heat. A few thrusts more and Mattie joins me, coating my insides with his seed — the hot flood almost enough to make me shoot again.

He collapses on top of me, sweaty forehead pressed against sweat-slickened back, plying me with kisses as he pulls out, his softened cock slipping easily from my hole. Too easily. And all at once, I'm feeling ravaged, empty, lost. I'm trembling with reaction like a junkie in withdrawal.

I miss him already — so fucking much. I'm stunned by the magnitude of my loss, by the immense, unfathomable, unbearable extent of it. My chest is too tight. I can't breathe — might never breathe again. The sob that tears from my throat burns like acid, like a million pieces of my heart have been ripped free.

There's only one thought left in my head: it's over. I've lost him. I'll never get past this, never recover from it, never, ever, ever be the same again.

# Chapter Thirteen

Mattie freezes. The kisses stop. His muscles tense. "Edge?" There's a hint of worry in his voice. "What is it? What's wrong?"

I can't answer. I shake my head. My body shudders from the force of all the sobs I'm holding back. But I will not cry in front of him, or with him, or...anywhere if it's at all possible. Even though I'm clearly open to doing more with him than I ever would have believed, I won't do that. Everyone has limits, after all.

"Edge?" The worried tone is more pronounced now. "Babe?" He moves to sit beside me, leaning over so he can look into my eyes. "*Michael?*"

I turn my head away. It's the only defense I have left. I'll lose it if I look at him. I'll shatter completely.

"Say something," Mattie whispers, stroking my head, my shoulder—finally shaking me to get my attention. "Please talk to me. Did I...did I hurt you? Edge...omigod... I am so, so sorry."

"Stop it!" I force myself to move, to push him aside and sit up. "You didn't hurt me, all right? I'm fine." I still can't look him in the eyes, but I also can't just lie here and let him think this mess is his fault either. Although in a way, of course, it really is.

"Well then, won't you at least tell me what I did?"

"Nothing." I take a deep breath and then another, force a small smile. "You didn't do anything, okay? It's just... Well, holy shit, that was one helluva good-bye fuck, wasn't it? Damn, babe. I guess you kind of took me by surprise. I wasn't expecting anything so… I mean, quite so…"

"G-good-bye?" His voice sounds plaintive. His fingers skate hesitantly over my thigh, igniting nerves I didn't even know I had—and every damn one of them connected to my heartstrings. "Wh-what are you talking about? Is there another assignment you have to take? Are you…are you leaving again? So soon?"

"Nope." I close my hand around his and squeeze it tight, partly just to hold on to it a little while longer, partly because he's killing me with his touch. "This has got nothing to do with me. I'm not going anywhere this time. You are. Congratulations, kid. You're being kicked upstairs."

"I-I'm…what?" He looks at me, puzzled, confused, worried. I want to erase that look. I want to take him in my arms and kiss him till he can't look anything but dazed and lust-struck.

"Now? Are you serious?" He shakes his head. "No. No way. I-I won't do it. I'm not going anywhere."

"Sure you are. Trust me, kid, once you've heard the news, there'll be no stopping you."

"I very much doubt it." Scowling, Mattie reclaims his hand and crosses his arms. "Now quit stalling and tell me what this is about. And don't call me kid."

I rake my fingers through my hair—anything to keep from taking back his hand—and take a few more deep breaths instead. It helps. A little. "Okay, look. On my last assignment I was sent to Santa Monica. There was a little girl with a high fever there. She'd had a seizure."

Mattie nods. "Yeah, that's rough. I used to get those too when I was a kid."

"That's what I figured. I knew it was probably hereditary. You don't have to worry though. She pulled through. She's gonna be okay."

Mattie's brow furrows in confusion. "Okay. That's nice, but...I don't even know her. Why would I be worried? And why are we talking about her now, anyway?"

"Because she's the point of all this. She's your daughter, Mattie. You have a little girl. Cute thing too."

The confused look intensifies. "She's my...what?"

"Your daughter. Yours and Meg's. And Beth's too, of course." Gotta give the girl her due, after all.

"I don't understand. What are you saying? Are you saying you saw Meg?"

"Saw her, talked to her, asked her about her daughter—found out who the father was. You did it, kid. I'm guessing she must have gotten pregnant right before you died. She probably didn't even know at the time. I mean, unless they've got some newfangled medical procedures going on now that I don't know about."

"And... Well...how is she? They. How are they?"

"They're good. Better anyway—now. Meg still misses you like crazy, of course, but she has Beth to see her through the difficult parts, which is how it should be. They got married. Did you know that?"

Mattie shakes his head. "No, I... Well, good. Good for them."

"Yep." I have to smile at that. "That's just what I said too."

"But... The baby. What about her? Is she gonna

be all right? You...you said she was sick?"

"Yeah, she was. But it's like I told you, there's nothing for you to worry about. She'll get better and...she's got two parents who love her. They're a family, Mattie." *And you're dead.*

No, I don't say that to him! Give me some credit. I think it, but... Anyway, I don't need to say it because he knows. I can see it on his face. "You have to let go now."

He nods, his face pensive. "I know."

"You don't want to be holding them back, right? They have to get on with their own lives. It's time."

"Stop it," he snaps, frowning angrily at me. "Enough already. You think you're telling me something I haven't figured out on my own?" I wait. Eventually his scowl fades. He nods again. "I got it, okay?"

"Yeah. Okay. So anyhow, I fibbed a little," I tell him. "When I was talking to them. I let them think you were already up in heaven watching over them all. So unless you want to make a liar out of me, you pretty much have to go now, don't you?"

"Is that true?" His eyes light up. I think I've finally piqued his interest. "I mean what you just said. Could I really do that? I mean if I were in heaven, could I watch over people and see what they're up to...stuff like that?"

I shrug. "Well, I haven't been, so I can't really say for certain, but it's what I've always heard." The top-echelon angels who pass through here now and then have always implied as much—the thrones and dominions and whatnot. Of course, that could just apply to them for all I know, and they're as different from us as the proverbial chalk and cheese.

I let Mattie process the information I've given him, then add, "There's more. Apparently you, my man, are a hero. You died saving someone's life. I guess you must have forgotten to mention that part of the story when you were telling me about it, huh?"

That last bit comes out sounding a little more bitter than I'd like, but I can't help it. I'm feeling bitter. I never would have gotten involved with him if I'd known at the start how hopelessly mismatched we were. I'm paying the price now for my ignorance, and it's far steeper than I'd ever imagined.

Mattie rubs the back of his neck. "I-I didn't know. No one ever told me what happened to her. I hoped she was okay, but... How did you find out?"

"Meg told me. It seems the woman tracked her down at your funeral. She wanted to make sure the present you'd bought got delivered. So you see? You did good with your life. You helped people. You made a difference. Maybe your life wasn't as long as you wanted, maybe you didn't plan for it to end the way it did, but you didn't just throw it away. You made your death count for something. There are people down there who will never forget you, people who wouldn't even be alive right now if it weren't for you. You've got nothing to regret, nothing to reproach yourself for. You've got no reason to stay here any longer."

I avert my eyes as I speak, because I know what happens next—what always happens when one of us ascends. They glow with an unbearable brightness, so filled with light it hurts to look at them. By the time the light fades and you can see again...they're gone, leaving nothing behind but a faint scent of roses. I have a strong suspicion I'm going to hate that particular fragrance from now on.

I need to take another deep breath and steel myself before continuing. I'm pleased that my voice remains steady as I say, "It's been an honor knowing you, Matteo Matinucci, but it's time for you to move on now, angel. It's time for you to go home."

"Oh, Edge..." Mattie's voice is soft—half-reproachful, half-amused. I try hard to ignore what it does to me. "Would you look at me, please?"

I shake my head, but he takes my chin in his hand, turning me to face him. I squint cautiously. No glow yet, but he's smiling so sweetly and he's so damn gorgeous it hurts to look at him all the same.

"I'm not going anywhere. You got that? Not without you. I'm not even leaving this room unless you come with me."

I sigh. "Appreciate it. Really I do. But you know that's not how it works." All the same, I take his hand and squeeze it tight. It feels good to be able to hold on to him a little while longer. It feels good to pretend things could work that way—just this once—that he could stay here. With me. Unfortunately, I know better.

"We each have to earn our own way out of limbo, Matt, and I'm not even close."

"Well then, what do you need to get you there? Tell me, and maybe I can help you find it, or figure it out, or whatever."

"No."

"No? Just like that?" Mattie quirks an eyebrow at me. "Back to that now, are we?" He slips his hand from mine and collapses back on the bed, the mattress bouncing a little beneath his weight. "Well, fine, then."

Yawning, he covers his head with a pillow. "Have it your way. Wake me when you're ready to move on. I'll just take a little nap while I'm waiting."

"Mattie..." I stare at him helplessly. "There are rules, you know—even here. Things are the way they are for a reason. You can't go around changing them to suit yourself just because you want to."

"Oh no?" He lifts the pillow and grins wickedly. "Watch me."

"Stop it." I reach over and snatch the pillow away, then lean down and kiss him hard. We're both still naked, and the temptation to postpone the inevitable just a little longer is nearly overwhelming. I want him bad. I'm so hungry for him it hurts. He snakes his arm around my neck, and it takes everything I have to pull back, to not get carried away. "I love you, Mattie, and God knows I want to spend eternity with you, but that's not our choice to make."

Technically, I suppose that's not completely true. I guess he could choose to defy the natural order of things, be like one of the angels who fell for the "daughters of men" and fathered the nephilim. But look how well that worked out.

Heaven doesn't come along every day. If he squanders this chance, if he wastes it on me, thinking it's only a matter of time before I'm ready to make the leap, how long will it be before I disappoint him? Before he realizes his mistake? Before he starts to resent me?

"Face it, Mattie, you just don't belong here anymore."

"Maybe you don't belong here anymore either," he says softly.

My guts are knotted with guilt and self-loathing as I twist away from him. "Maybe you're right. Maybe I never should have been sent here at all." I always figured you had to have screwed up in some more or less major way in order to get stuck here—maybe not quite as badly as I did, but at least a little. As far as "feel good" ideas go, it wasn't great, but it did give me hope. It took Mattie to prove that theory wrong. If he didn't get into heaven on the first shot, what are my chances of ever making the grade?

Mattie sits up and drapes an arm around my shoulders. "Talk to me, babe. Tell me what's wrong."

I lean into him, shameless in my need. "You're never gonna stop pestering me about this, are you?"

"Sure I will. If you'd just answer the question, I wouldn't have to ask it again."

"No, you'll just ask something else."

His arm tightens around me. "That is a distinct possibility." He chuckles quietly. His warm breath tickles my ear. My heart clenches.

Why can't he let me be? Why can't he just…leave? He's supposed to go. Why can't he ever do what he's supposed to do? Why can't he simply follow orders?

I freeze as I hear my own thoughts. Dear God, I sound just like Lorraine. I suppose that's what gives me the idea. I hate the idea of hurting him, but really, what else can I do? And what does it matter at this point, anyway? Sometimes things end badly because that's the only way they can end.

I pull away from him and get off the bed. "Fine, then. You really want to know? I decided to test out your theory about Lorraine. I spoke with her when I got back from Earth. I told her I wanted to see if the two of us couldn't work things out."

"And?" He looks surprised and more than a little pleased. His lips twitch as though he's trying hard not to smile, as though he thinks he knows what's coming next. But I know how to fix that.

I shrug disinterestedly. "And...apparently we could. Getting her to take me back wasn't as hard as I thought it would be."

"Take you back?" His smile is a distant memory now. I should be happy about that, I guess. "What does that mean?"

"Oh, don't act like you're surprised," I tell him. "You knew I'd only been with women before you. You had to know it was only a matter of time before I'd go back to...to what I was used to. To what I really wanted all along."

"What are you saying?" He surges off the bed, staring at me, looking hurt and bewildered.

"Lorraine and I, we had a thing. We were an item. A couple. We...dated."

"Did you sleep with her?"

I drop my gaze. "Don't act surprised." I'm repeating myself, but I can't seem to help that. "What did you expect? I told you all along I wasn't gay. Besides, what's the difference? You're leaving anyway."

"I wasn't leaving," he says quietly. "I told you that. I told you I didn't want to go anywhere without you."

I glare at him then. "And I told you that's not an option. There's no reason for you to stay here, Mattie. This is not where you belong." We stare at each other for a moment, but it's a moment too long. I have to look away. "Just let it go," I tell him. "Just get the fuck out of here." This time he does. In the time it takes my heart to clench, he wavers out of sight.

I'm relieved for half a second. Mostly relieved, anyway. Relief mixed with shame, with longing, with regret. I wish I could have handled things better. But then the other shoe falls. I've screwed up. I don't know why it takes me so long to realize it. There'd been no glow, no heat, no flash of light. No roses.

There'd been nothing to indicate that Mattie had moved on to heaven.

*Because he didn't, you fucking idiot.*

I don't know what the hell I could have been thinking. Was I that caught up in my own selfish feelings—again? How could I have imagined it would be possible to use pain to push someone at heaven, when heaven is the absence of pain? At best, Mattie's gone somewhere to cool off, to lick his wounds, consider his next move. At worst...he's off doing something we'll both regret, something that will keep him stuck here for who knows how long and make him hate me even more than he already does.

# Chapter Fourteen

They say it's a sure sign of insanity when you keep doing the same things over and over again, expecting the outcome to be different, but I think sometimes it's just a matter of old habits being hard to break. At least that's what I tell myself when I go in search of Sophia. There's really nothing insane about it anyway. She'd always been my friend and mentor; that's exactly what I need right now. End of story.

Of course, it's not really the end. I realize that when I track her down. She's at the lake where I first saw Mattie. If the location surprises me, I'm even more surprised when I realize she's not alone. When I realize the identity of the person huddled with her at the end of the pier, relief crashes through me. "Mattie?"

He glances up, startled, his eyes swimming with tears — just as they'd been when we first met. He turns away. Wrapping his arms around himself, he stares out across the lake.

Beating back my initial disappointment, I breathe a sigh of relief. Perhaps I've gotten lucky. Perhaps I've caught him before things have gone too far wrong. As I watch, Sophia disengages herself and turns away from Mattie. She's glaring as she walks toward me. Anger ripples around her like a heat mirage, and I swear the force of her fury nearly knocks me off balance. I have to brace myself just to stay on my feet and avoid going into the water.

"What have you done?" she demands quietly once she's reached my side. "You and Lorraine? Again? Really? Because things weren't already complicated enough?"

"Of course not." I might be insane, but I'm not that insane. "You know me better'n that, don't you? I just figured if he thought I was involved with someone else—that I'd moved on—it would be easier for him to move on as well. He has to go, Soph. I may not like it, but you know I'm right."

Sophia sighs. I can feel some of the anger leave her. "Oh, Edge."

"I told you this would happen, didn't I? Didn't I tell you I'd screw this up?"

"Never mind what you told me. All you need to worry about right now is what you're going to tell him." She jerks her head in Mattie's direction. "Fix this," she hisses just before she disappears. "And don't give me any more nonsense about not knowing how. You know everything you need to know. You always have. Stop stalling."

Mattie continues to ignore me as I join him at the end of the pier. I place a hand on his shoulder. He flinches at the touch.

"I'm sorry," I tell him. "I didn't mean it. You know that, don't you?"

"It isn't supposed to be this way," he says, his voice a cracked whisper. He thumps the middle of his chest with his clenched fist. "Love...it was never supposed to hurt like this."

I can't think of anything to say to that, so I don't. What am I supposed to tell him? That this isn't how I ever imagined things would turn out for me either? Trust me, it's not.

Mattie turns toward the shore. He studies the cottage, which is once again in its picture-perfect, prefire incarnation. "You know, it's funny that I ended up here," he says, his voice still thick with pain. "Because this is where it happened, where I lost my faith. Where I figured out that nothing lasts. People die, they leave you...and that's pretty much the only thing you can count on." He shakes his head. "I thought I was over that. I thought I'd made my peace with the past, but then you came along. You made me believe again. In love. In you..."

He looks at me. In his eyes, I see an infinite world of pain. Enough to make me drop my gaze.

"You made me believe in all the stupid shit I thought I'd never believe in again. Do you know how that made me feel—to realize I'd been so wrong?"

I shrug helplessly. "I just wanted you to be happy."

"Happy?" He stares at me in disbelief. "You think I'm happy knowing you're so miserable you'd resort to lying just to get rid of me? "

"I wasn't thinking straight, all right? The thought of losing you... That hurts so much, I still can't think straight. I love you, Mattie, but I won't keep you here. You can hate me or not—that's your choice—but I won't be the reason you stay."

He studies me for a moment, then shrugs. "It's my choice too, isn't it?" he says as he reaches for me.

"Yeah, but it's a bad choice," I protest even as I cling to him. "It's not worth it. I'm not worth it."

"That's your opinion. As it happens, I disagree."

Perfect. We're right back where we started. I rack my brain for anything I can use to make my point. "I'm not like you, Mattie," I tell him finally. "When I was alive...I wasn't brave or courageous. I never had the guts to come clean about who and what I was, not even to myself."

"You mean about being gay?"

I shake my head, but I'm too tired to argue the point anymore. What difference does it make? "Okay, fine. We didn't call it that, but yes, I suppose. I couldn't accept being...different in that way. I didn't want to accept it. I did everything I could to deny it. I even got married—holy matrimony, no chance of a divorce—because it wasn't bad enough that my life was screwed up. I had to ruin hers as well."

Mattie gives my shoulders a squeeze. "Easy there, babe. I'm sure you were doing the best you could."

"Well, my best wasn't very good, was it? There's no making excuses for it. I was selfish and weak. I hurt people—all to save face, to preserve the fiction that I was normal. And in the end...it didn't even matter. I threw my life away, and it all came out. It was all for nothing."

"You know, you never did tell me how you died." He tosses the question off nonchalantly. And oh, yes, it is a question—don't let his phrasing of it fool you.

I know a moment of panic. Surely it won't come down to that? I don't want to answer. I don't want him to know. I don't want to give up any more of my self-respect, and I sure as hell don't want to lose what little there might be left of his regard for me. Haven't I already lost enough? But he's never going to let it go, and he deserves the truth.

Besides, I figure I've wasted enough people's chances at happiness already. I can't have him sacrificing himself on my account. I really can't.

I look away. I wish we were back at my beach so that when he leaves—when he recoils in disgust and deserts me—I can lose myself for a time contemplating the wind and the waves. So I can pretend I'm content in my solitude rather than being here, where everything is a reminder of our time together, where every instant alone will be torture.

"Edge?" he prompts when I'm quiet too long.

"I killed myself. All right? Are you happy now?"

"Not really. Why'd you do it? Did you mean to, or was it an accident?"

I stare at him, almost too shocked to speak. What does he know? Who's he been talking to? "What the hell is that supposed to mean?"

Matteo shrugs. "It's just a question."

"It sure as hell is not just a question! Besides, I think I've answered enough of your questions."

I push myself out of his arms and turn away. He says nothing, but I can feel him watching me.

"Did you hear what I said?" I ask when I can no longer stand the silence.

"I heard you. I'm just choosing to ignore it. Did you leave a note?"

That makes me laugh. "No. I didn't bother with a note. The only thing I left behind was my body—hanging right where my wife was sure to find it, as if I hadn't already caused her enough hurt and shame."

"I'm sorry," he says quietly. "That must have been very hard for her. I understand why you would feel bad about something like that, but it's not like you meant for it to happen that way, right?"

I whirl around to face him. "Of course I didn't mean for it to…" Awareness hits me. I've been tricked.

"Very clever," I mutter, closing my eyes in defeat. "Okay, fine. No, I did not plan on killing myself. All right? I didn't mean for any of it to happen. It just...did."

Mattie nods. "Right. Kind of like what happened to me."

"No." I glare at him. "Not like you. Nothing at all like you. I didn't give my life to save someone else's. There was nothing heroic about my death."

"Don't overdramatize things," he says as he gathers me close once again. "A car jumped the curb and ran me down. My death was an accident—pure and simple. Just like my family's deaths. Just like yours."

I shake my head. There was nothing pure or simple about the way I died. It was loathsome. Shameful. "Your family was taken by surprise, and you...you didn't even know that woman, yet you sacrificed yourself for her."

"I didn't intend to. It was a reflex. She wasn't moving. I gave her a push. If I'd known how it would turn out...who knows what I would have done."

I know. I know exactly what he would have done. He'd have done the right thing, the brave thing. Not the chickenshit thing. "Why are you doing this?"

"Because I love you," he says, brushing a gentle kiss against my lips. "Because I can see how much you're hurting, and I want to help."

I know I probably shouldn't kiss him back. I do it anyway. I even try briefly to convince myself that making love to him again—one last time—will make it that much easier for us both to say good-bye. But even I'm not that delusional. Yet.

If he stays here even a little longer, however, all bets are off.

"Let it go, Matteo," I beg, breaking the kiss. "Please."

"Mattie," he corrects gently. "And I tell you what. If you'll stop calling me Matteo, I promise I won't call you Michael...much."

"Matteo," I repeat stubbornly. I need the formality. It's the only boundary I have left at this point.

"Whatever." He kisses me again, even more tenderly. "Tell me what happened."

Getting Mattie closure was supposed to be simple. I'm still not sure where things started going wrong. How did it end up being so hard? How did it end up costing me so much? I groan against his mouth as despair melds with longing and flows straight into surrender.

How did it end up costing me everything?

I rest my head on his shoulder—just so I don't have to look into his face as I tell him the truth, things I've never confided to another soul. "I couldn't get what I needed from my marriage, sexually speaking. I was miserable, frustrated, and my wife... Well, I don't suppose it was very good for her either. But I didn't care. I was so fucking selfish. She knew I wasn't satisfied with what we had. She thought it was her fault, and I let her. I let her think my disappointment with her was forcing me to go elsewhere for gratification—to other partners."

"And did you?"

I shrug. "No. What would have been the point? I'd been with other women before we married. That had been even less satisfying. And I wouldn't admit my attraction to men. I'd only ever allow myself to think about it as part of a fantasy. Even then I wasn't altogether comfortable with it. But I had a workshop behind the house, and I used to shut myself in there for hours and...take care of things myself. Most of the time I'd wait until she was off doing the marketing or visiting one of her girlfriends. I didn't want to risk being discovered. I had a trunk where I kept my equipment locked up: ropes, special clothing I liked to use—women's clothing—and various restraints."

Mattie sighs. "I suppose you're talking about autoerotic asphyxia, aren't you?" he asks as he strokes his fingers through my hair.

I squeeze my eyes closed—as if there was the slightest chance of shutting out either the memories or the questions. "It had to be forbidden, you know? Even in fantasy I couldn't accept it other than as something I was forced into. That's how it started. After a while...I needed it. I couldn't seem to get satisfaction any other way."

"So what happened?"

"I don't know. I was usually very careful, but obviously this one time... I guess I wasn't careful enough. Maybe I was rushing. Maybe I was looking for a way to punish myself. Maybe I couldn't stand it anymore and I really did kill myself. What difference does it make?"

"Easy," Mattie whispers, pressing a kiss against my head. "Don't push it. Just let it out."

"I didn't even realize I was dead at first. I don't know for how long, but I guess it must have been a while. I was still there—still hanging around in spirit—

when my wife got one of our neighbors to help her break the door down. She was afraid something had happened to me, but...she wasn't expecting to find me like that." My face burns as I remember the scene, the look of horror on her face. My stomach roils in disgust. I was lucky not to have become a ghost at that point, not to have become trapped there by shame and despair. I was damned lucky.

The thought strikes me as so ironic I start to laugh. Me — one of the lucky ones — who'd a thunk it?

"What's so funny?" Mattie asks softly. But how the hell do I explain something like that?

I steal a look at his face. He's smiling gently at me — an invitation to share the joke. "All of it, I guess," I tell him with a shrug. Then I flash on something he'd said to me back in the beginning, and I smile too. "Just all the blue and green of it. You know? From this distance...it really doesn't matter. Maybe it never did."

"It was an accident," Mattie says, gazing at me expectantly, awaiting my response.

I nod. "Yes."

"It wasn't your fault."

"Well..." That one's harder. No way near as cut-and-dried. It was I who'd tied the knots, after all.

"Edge..."

"Okay, fine." I sigh in surrender. "It wasn't my fault."

"You were a victim of the culture you grew up in. You were a victim of a repressive society that wouldn't let you be who you were."

I look away, laughing. Yep, that's me. Lucky. Not a ghost. Society's victim. I'm a mess is what I am. A not-so-pretty combination of contradictions. A veritable tuna casserole of clichés.

"I like that," Mattie murmurs as he pulls me closer, flush against him, chest to chest, groin to groin, heart to heart.

"What?" I ask as I wrap my arms around his waist. Who cares if it's just for a moment? Every moment counts, doesn't it?

"You. Laughing. I like that a lot."

So do I, come to think of it. It feels good. He dips his head and kisses me. I close my eyes and kiss him back. No hesitation. No second thoughts. No regrets. Screw salvation, you know? And screw eternity too. This is good. I'm good. Right here, right now, I'm happy.

I feel the love and light radiating from Mattie, and I open my heart and take it all in. It's part of me...or I'm part of it. I'm not real certain which is which, but I'm pretty sure that doesn't matter either. It's all the same. I don't even flinch when I feel it all start to blur and dissolve, when I know it's all about to end. It was worth it. I feel only gratitude—gratitude and love.

In the next instant, there's a rush of heat that seems to flood through every cell at once. I try and catch my breath, and when that's not possible, I just give in and let that go as well.

Blue and green. Black-and-white. Light and dark. It really is all the same. It's all okay. It all just is...

# Chapter Fifteen

I have no idea where I am when I open my eyes again. Seriously. No idea. None. Perhaps that's because nothing looks even remotely familiar...or even remotely like any *thing* at all. I'm surrounded by shades of light or shades of bright or something even more vague. I look around curiously, nearly jumping out of my skin when I feel something brush against my shoulder.

I spin around, then sigh in relief. "You," I whisper, gazing happily at Mattie.

"Me," he says, flashing a slightly goofy smile that's gotta be the hottest thing I've ever seen. And yeah, I know, goofy doesn't usually rank high on the sexy scale with me either, but I'm weird, okay? I figured that was a given by now.

"So...where the fuck are we?" I tear my gaze from his face long enough for another sweep of our all-but-nonexistent environment.

Mattie tsk-tsks in mock annoyance. "Show a little respect, can't you? That's a fine way for an angel to describe his first view of heaven."

"Heaven? You're shitting me, right? It can't be." I look around again. On the other hand... Hell, what do I know? Maybe it is. "But how?"

"Closure, babe." Mattie smiles fondly at me. "That was all you ever needed."

I shake my head. "No way. That's not right. That can't be..." I had way more than that on my plate. I know it. I had sins I was certain I'd never be able to atone for. Another suspicion nags at me. "Wait, this wasn't all about me...was it?"

"This?"

"You. Me meeting you. Everything we did together."

"Not all about you, no."

I'm suddenly filled with foreboding, chilled to the bone. "Mattie..."

"Okay, mostly it was, I suppose, but not all. Some of it was definitely about me too."

"You tricked me." I'm not quite sure how I feel about that—a little dismayed I suppose, but beyond that...

"Well, someone had to do something," another voice chimes in.

I turn to find Sophia beaming at me. I feel even more confused. "Soph...how did you get here?"

"I've always been able to come here," she says, smiling sweetly at me. "I told you I'd been in limbo from the start. I choose to stay there because there are so many worthy souls who need my help. You, however, needed something more than I could give you."

"Which is why you sent Mattie. Not for me to help him, but for him to help me." My voice sounds lifeless and dull, and I'm feeling way beyond dismayed at this point. "I guess ignorance really is bliss." If this is heaven, I'm highly disappointed. I knew I shoulda stayed in limbo.

"Edge, it wasn't like that," Mattie says. "Really." He lays a hand on my arm, but I can't face him.

"Did you ever actually love me at all?" I ask, the words slipping out before I have time to consider how very much I don't want to know the answer to that particular question. "Or was it all just part of the job to you?"

"What? Of course I love you! You know I do. How can you even ask?"

He sounds near tears himself, but I'm not sure I buy it. I'm beginning to suspect it was no accident he'd been living in LA at the time of his death. Was he really going to be a doctor, or did he just want to play one on TV?

"Sophia, tell him," Mattie says pleadingly.

"Michael Alphonse Edge," Sophia snaps, making me cringe with her use of my full name. Is it any wonder I've chosen to forgo given names? "Stop being so defensive. Of course Mattie loves you. Why else would he have chosen to leave heaven for your sake if he didn't care?"

"I don't know." I'm trying hard to feel grateful — the way I was feeling just a moment ago. I'm trying hard to feel loved and cherished and accepted. But I don't. I just feel lost instead. Lost. Alone. Betrayed. I want *my* Mattie back, the Mattie I thought I knew, not this…this *impostor*.

And yes, it takes me just that long for Sophia's words to sink in. "Wait… What you just said…" I turn to Mattie, glare at him accusingly. "You've been here already? Before I even knew you?" Now I know for certain it was all just a game to him. No wonder he was so damned good at everything, so gifted. I turn my back on him. Maybe they're both still lying to me. Maybe this isn't heaven at all. At the moment, it's feeling suspiciously like hell.

"Edge," Mattie whispers pleadingly, but I shake my head. I won't turn around. I won't let him see what he's done to me, how destroyed I've become. I was so in love with him. I'm still so in love with him. And I can't regret a minute of the time we spent together. But I bared my heart and my soul to him—I gave him everything he wanted. Why couldn't he at least have let me keep the illusion that he loved me too?

Sophia sighs. "You were right about at least one thing, Edge. Mattie hadn't done anything so terrible that it would have kept him out of heaven. He had a few closure issues that needed to be dealt with—just as you clearly do right now—but he could have taken care of all that here. In fact, it would have been easier to deal with them here. This is a higher plane, after all; it lends itself to that kind of perspective. But once he'd gotten a glimpse of limbo—a glimpse of you—he fell. He couldn't bear watching you suffer. He chose to go to limbo to be with you, hoping that the two of you could be a help to each other."

Typical Mattie, I think as I shake my head. Meg was right. Apparently he always does have to be a hero.

"I know you think everyone lied to you," Sophia continues. "But I promise you that wasn't the case. When Mattie arrived in limbo, his memory was wiped. He had no recollection of his time on this plane, no recollection of having made the decision to leave heaven. As far as you or he or almost anyone else there knew, he was newly dead. Everything that occurred between the two of you was genuine and authentic. That's the only way it could have worked. And if you had failed to help him win his way back here, or if he couldn't have turned things around for you, he could very well have become trapped there, just as surely as you were, with very little hope of ever finding his way back. I have to tell you, I was not in favor of the scheme. For a while it looked like it was touch and go. We weren't sure if either of you was going to make it."

"How could you have let him do that?" I demand, furious with her on his behalf. Even I'm not that selfish, and I figure that's saying something. "How could you let him make that kind of mistake?"

"How could I have stopped him," Sophia asks gently. "When he was acting out of love? It might not always work out the way we hope it will, but love is never a mistake."

Heart clenching, I turn at last to Mattie. "You did that...for me?"

His eyes are brimming with tears, just as they were the first time I saw him. "I love you, Edge. I have from the start. I would have done anything to help you. You have to know that."

I nod. "I do," I say—and mean it. I reach for his hand and pull him into my arms. He melts against me with a muffled sob. Our lips meet in the wettest kiss I've ever known, with both of us in tears. I break it off to try and kiss the teardrops from his face, but that only makes him cry harder.

Never let them tell you there are no tears in heaven. I know for a fact that's not the case.

The tears are falling too fast for me to wipe away, and some of them are mine. I give up finally and simply hold him close. "I'm sorry I doubted you," I whisper as I rock him gently in my arms. "I'm sorry for everything. I love you too, you know. Always will."

Sophia sighs—a soft, contented sound. "Well, that's better. And now I think I'll leave you two children alone for a while."

"Wait." I struggle to disentangle myself as she starts to turn away. She pauses, waiting for me, but then I can't find the words to express all the gratitude in my heart. Apparently, I don't have to. I guess maybe that's one of the perks of being in heaven.

Sophia smiles. "You're very welcome, love."

"Will we ever see you again?" I ask.

She looks surprised. "Well, of course you will. As often as you want. Why would that have changed?"

"So...okay, but...what do we do now?" This is all so new to me. It's been so long since I was the newbie. So very long. Surely I can be excused for feeling a little bit lost—right? Even here.

Sophia shakes her head, eyes gleaming with amusement. "This is heaven," she says, turning away once more. Laughter shimmers in her voice. "You can do whatever you like. But don't worry, Edge. When you're ready for them, there will be lots of exciting assignments waiting for you. By now we're all very well aware of your low threshold for boredom."

I glance meaningfully at Mattie. "Maybe not so much anymore," I say, enchanted by the embarrassed blush that stains his cheeks.

The echo of Sophia's laughter lingers in the ether for several moments after she fades from view, but finally we're alone.

"So..." I say as I wrap an arm around Mattie's waist and pull him close.

He drapes his arms over my shoulders and smiles back, brown eyes glowing with love. "So...?"

"What do you want to do first?"

His smile widens. "Well, I don't know...Alphonse. What do *you* want to do first?"

"Don't," I say, wincing a little at the name. "Just don't, okay?" Sheesh. I'm thinking the boy could use another of those convenient memory wipes right about now.

"Whatever you say," he murmurs, but his demure tone doesn't fool me for an instant. I'm in for a world of teasing. An eternity of teasing.

Which doesn't sound half-bad, if you must know.

I sigh. "Just shut up and kiss me." But before he can, I'm hit by an awful thought. "Oh no."

"What now?" Mattie pulls back, gazing worriedly at me. "Edge? What's wrong?"

"Well, we're in heaven, right?" Suddenly, I'm feeling more than a little unsure. "So...what does that mean? Do angels kiss in heaven? Or does this mean...no more sex?"

Mattie laughs, joy and relief mingling on his face. "Why would you even think such a thing?" he asks as he fixes me with a look that's hot enough to incinerate planets.

It's a good thing we don't really need to breathe, 'cause I swear I've forgotten how. I'm hit by a wave of déjà vu. I thought I was in trouble the first time I saw him; now I know what real trouble is: it's everything that look in his eyes is promising. And I want it. Oh do I want it.

"That's right, baby," Mattie says with a smile so mocking it can only mean he's reading my mind. "And I'm going to give it to you." He snaps his fingers, and just like that, our clothes disappear.

I swallow hard. "I want to learn to do that."

"I'll teach you." He leans in and presses a tender

kiss against my lips. I swear I feel invisible hands touching me everywhere, tweaking my nipples, caressing my balls. "There's so much I'm gonna show you."

"I'd like that." I think somewhere along the line our roles have gotten reversed, but I'm cool with that. Giving up control—sometimes it's not as hard as you think.

"Oh, you'll more than like it," he promises laughingly.

As Mattie's fingers trace lightly over my face, they leave a trail of something cool, wet, and tingling in their wake. I brush at my cheek and then stare at my hand in surprise. "Lube?"

Mattie grins wickedly. He holds up his hand and shows me his fingers, slick, glistening, coated with gel. "Convenient, don't you think?"

I nod, but the only thing I'm really thinking about is where he plans on sticking those fingers. My ass clenches. My heart pounds. My mouth goes dry. *Hell yes.* "Fuck, Mattie."

"Getting to that."

He tugs me close and kisses me again. Really kisses me this time, with one hand fisted in my hair, the other teasing the crack of my ass. I clutch his shoulders. I'm so dizzy with lust I can't stand it. His finger penetrates me, and I whimper with need. I'm afraid I might pass out, and a small part of me has to wonder if perhaps he's doing that on purpose. Is this payback for what I did to Beth?

But thinking about that leads to thoughts of Lorraine—and that outfit she was wearing last time I saw her.

"You really have to stop thinking about girls," Mattie says as he pulls back to look at me, and I can't tell if he's teasing or not. "You thinking you're straight—that's a holdover from another lifetime."

He has to be teasing. Right? I lick my lips, stalling for time as I organize my thoughts. Sometimes it's not enough to know something is true. Sometimes you need to say the words out loud. "I know that. And I promise I'm not thinking of anyone but you. I love you, Mattie."

"And I love you." He smiles tenderly at me. "And that's the whole point of heaven, isn't it? I can't think of anything more heavenly than making love to you for all eternity."

That makes two of us. I'm smiling as I draw him to me once more—this time forever. "Amen to that."

# About the Author

PG Forte inhabits a world only slightly less strange than the ones she creates. Filled with serendipity, coincidence, love at first sight and dreams come true...it also bears an uncanny resemblance to Berkeley, California.

She wrote her first serialized story when she was still in her teens. The sexy, ongoing adventure tales were very popular at her oh-so-proper, all girls, Catholic High School, where they helped to liven up otherwise dull classes. Even if her teachers didn't always think so.

Originally a Jersey girl, PG now resides on the extreme left coast where she writes rule bending, genre blending erotic romance and paranormal stories.

When she's not pestering her husband to help her research scenes for upcoming books, she can usually be found serving the needs and whims of her characters....or her pets. It's a difficult job, but someone's got to do it.

## Links to reach PG Forte:

www.PGForte.com
Facebook.com/AuthorPGForte
Twitter.com/PGForte